LANTERN PRESS BOOKS

are complete and unabridged reprints of titles in the several series of thematic short-story anthologies published originally by Lantern Press, Inc. Over two million copies have been sold in their higher-priced, cloth-bound editions.

Teachers, librarians, and reviewers have often recommended these carefully edited anthologies. For instance, *Scholastic Teacher* said: "All are suitable as supplementary readers for junior high school students. Each title appears on most school and library approved reading lists and is recommended by *The Library Journal*. Though mainly for junior high school readers, they can be read with pleasure by older students and they are endorsed by Spache in GOOD READING FOR POOR READERS."

A complete list of the titles now available will be found on the reverse side of this page. If your bookseller doesn't have a title you want, you can get it by sending retail price, local sales tax if any, plus 25¢ per book for postage and handling to Mail Service Department, Pocket Books, a Division of Simon & Schuster, Inc., 1 West 39th Street, New York, N.Y. 10018. If you are ordering for delivery in Canada, send retail price plus 25¢ per book for postage and handling to Simon & Schuster of Canada, Ltd., 225 Yonge Street North, Richmond Hill, Ontario. In either case, please send check or money order. We cannot be responsible for cash.

SUSPENSE STORIES

Edited by
A. L. FURMAN

ORIGINAL TITLE: *Teen-Age Suspense Stories*

A LANTERN
PRESS BOOK

PUBLISHED BY POCKET BOOKS NEW YORK

SUSPENSE STORIES

Lantern Press Book edition published 1967

6th printing .... October, 1976

ISBN: 0-671-75747-4.

To all the contributing authors of these suspense stories with sincere appreciation for their co-operation.

Contents

Suspense Stories

The Best of
All Possible Worlds

◆━━━━━━◆━━━━━━◆

LORETTA STREHLOW

AS Sue Sterns stepped onto the curb, the dark police car pulled alongside and lanky Bruce Wells slid out to tower above her. Leaning over, Sue greeted the pleasant faced officer in the driver's seat.

"Morning, Captain Wells. Still driving your lazy son to work, I see."

"Well, it's on my way and poor company is better than none," Bruce's father laughed as he pulled away from the curb.

"Speaking about being lazy . . ." Bruce consulted his watch. "What brings you downtown so early this Friday morning? Must be all of quarter to nine."

"I've finally found a job."

Seventeen-year-old Sue spoke with relief. Jobs

1

in Bartonville, especially summer jobs, weren't so easy to find with all the teenagers competing for the few available. Bruce had been lucky. He'd worked behind the soda fountain at Couglin's drugstore since they'd been juniors and after June graduation Mr. Couglin had put him on full time, not, Sue thought, because the fountain was so busy but because he knew Bruce would need the money for college that fall. Sue and Bruce and half of their graduating class planned to go on to State in September. Sue had saved baby-sitting money and the little she'd earned ushering at the theatre before it closed but she'd counted on a summer job to fill in the gaps in her wardrobe and help pay the tuition.

"Who got stuck?" Bruce asked grimly.

"Miss Ketter. I'm going to clerk for her."

"Ketter?"

"She's from the city. Bought Pearson's little gift shop."

Bruce groaned. "Well, tell Miss Ketter that with you working for her she's going to find out that this is the best of all possible worlds."

He neatly avoided the kick Sue aimed at his shin and disappeared into the drugstore. The best of all possible worlds, indeed. Sue giggled as she crossed the street. Ever since they'd read Voltaire's *Candide* in senior English she and Bruce had stolen the phrase when they meant just the opposite of what the words said. When Sue had caught the mumps

2

from her little brother and missed the senior prom, Bruce sent her corsage along with a note . . . To the best girl in the best of all possible worlds . . . and Sue, knowing what he'd meant, had smiled through her tears. Now they used the phrase whenever they meant that something disastrous was going to happen.

"I'll show Mr. Bruce Wells," Sue thought resolutely, wrinkling her nose at her reflection in the window of the hardware store. She spent a moment arranging her already neat brown bangs and straightening her suit jacket before turning to open the gift shop door. A little bell jangled above her and a beautifully coiffed blonde emerged from the back room.

"Good morning, Miss Ketter. I hope I'm not late."

"Not at all." The blonde woman hesitated. "Sue . . . isn't it?"

"Yes." Sue, standing awkwardly just inside the door, flushed and wished she'd worn something a little dressier than her old blue suit.

"Well, come in. Come in." Miss Ketter pointed a manicured finger at the jumble of boxes and cartons in the corner. "You can see there's still a lot to be done. We won't open officially until the first of next week."

Several hours later Sue had changed her mind. She wished she'd worn something more comfortable that was easier to clean than the suit with its long sleeves that seemed to wipe up as much dust as the cloth Sue used to clean the glass display shelves. The opening of the door set the bell to jingling again and the two women looked up to see a slender, dark haired man swing a suitcase through the door and walk toward them.

"Miss Ketter? I represent Archer Jewelry Sales. I thought you might be interested in our latest line."

For just a minute, Sue thought she detected annoyance in Miss Ketter's smooth face.

"It's almost eleven, Sue. Why don't you take an early lunch while I see if the gentleman has anything worthwhile."

Passing the hardware store, Sue realized she'd forgotten her purse. Turning, she stepped back into the gift shop.

"You fool! I can't take a chance. . . ." The bell shut off the rest of Miss Ketter's words but Sue had heard enough to know that she was very angry. She whirled on Sue. "I told you to go to lunch."

Sue flushed. The man had turned his back and was running a careless finger over one bare shelf.

"I left my purse."

Snatching it from behind the counter, Sue backed toward the door. She ran almost all the way to the drugstore and crept into a booth in the back. How could her first morning go so wrong? What had she done? She wished she didn't have to go

4

back but she knew she'd never find another job this late in the summer.

"You're early for lunch, aren't you?" Bruce leaned over the table. "Miss Ketter get rid of you already?"

"Of course not." Sue forced a smile. "She knows that I'm the best of all possible help."

Bruce dipped his head, his blue eyes serious. "Cheer up, Sue. The first day's always rough. How about a movie tonight to talk over the grim details?"

Sue agreed quickly and, after one of Bruce's just-right sandwiches, she went back to the shop. There was no sign of the salesman. Miss Ketter, her bland face calm again, was in the back room marking jewelry. She stood when Sue came in.

"I'm sorry I blew up, Sue. That jewelry salesman said something that irritated me but I told him . . ." She paused, running a finger through her silky hair. "Anyway, next time he'll know better. It had nothing to do with you and I apologize again."

Relieved, Sue nodded. The afternoon went much the same as the morning and by the time Bruce picked her up for the show that night she had nearly forgotten the incident. They drove to the nearby city of Melrose for the Friday night feature and afterwards stopped at one of the pizza places downtown. Sue was looking out the window when she saw them.

5

"That's funny."

Bruce looked up. "What's funny?"

Sue shook her head. "I'm almost sure I just saw Miss Ketter going into the Hotel Clinton across the street."

"Well, what's so strange about that?" Bruce asked. "I thought you told me she still lived here and commuted to the shop."

"She does. That's not what I mean, Bruce." Sue's brown eyes were puzzled. "She was with that man, that salesman who came in today."

"The one that upset her so?"

Sue nodded.

"Oh," Bruce shrugged, "probably just someone that looks like her . . . or him. Not too likely that she'd have a date with the guy after she talked to him the way you said she did."

"I suppose not," Sue agreed but she couldn't keep from watching the hotel steps as the people came and went.

Sue slept fitfully that night and rushed into the kitchen on Saturday morning, buttoning her blouse with one hand while she grabbed for juice with the other.

"I'll be late, Mom," Sue accused. "Why didn't you call me?"

Her mother's hand flew to her mouth. "I'm sorry, Sue. Your father and I got to talking about all those robberies and I forgot the time."

"What robberies?"

Her father glanced up from the paper. "Jewelry stores, galleries . . . in the city. Been three within the last month, the latest just last night. They got away with the private Crawford collection that was on loan to the museum."

"And not a trace of who's doing it," her mother spoke indignantly from the stove. "You'd think the police in a city as big as Melrose would be able to stop something like that."

"Oh, Mom, the stolen goods will turn up somewhere," Sue prophesied. "The police must have some leads."

Sue gulped her breakfast and hurried to work. The roller shade was still drawn when she arrived at the shop and the door, locked. Sue was about to turn away when she heard the click of heels and Miss Ketter, neatly dressed in flouncy skirt and expensive looking blouse, opened the door.

"Good morning, Sue." Her words were for Sue but her eyes still watched the stock room and, for an instant, Sue had the feeling that someone else was in the shop with them.

"Good morning, Miss Ketter." Stepping inside, Sue let the door click shut. At that same moment she thought she heard another door close and when the cool morning draft struck her ankles she was sure it had been the door leading to the narrow alley behind the shop. Probably a delivery man with more packages, Sue thought idly.

"It won't be necessary for you to have a key,

7

Sue," Miss Ketter said crisply. "Once we get organized here there will be some mornings when I won't come in until later but I'll arrange for you to take my key the night before. Besides," she shook her sleek head in exasperation, "the lock on the back door catches and can only be opened from the inside and I haven't had time to have another key made for the front door yet."

"What if . . ." Sue hesitated and then hurried on. "What if I need to get in touch with you about something? Can I reach you at the Clinton?"

"Why, yes . . ." Miss Ketter whirled to face Sue. "How did you know I'm staying at the Clinton?"

Sue felt her face glow red. "I was in the city last night. I saw you going into the hotel and just assumed . . ."

"Well, you're right," Miss Ketter's full lips made a thin smile, "I do live at the hotel but you were wrong about seeing me last night. I had a terrible headache and didn't leave my room at all once I got out of here." She waved a hand at the shop and its disorder of boxes and tissue wrappings. "I'm beginning to hate the sight of this place and we haven't even opened yet." She shrugged one slim shoulder and turned to the back room. "You can finish stocking the shelves . . . use your own judgment. I'm going out for some coffee and then I'll be marking things in the back room."

8

After Miss Ketter had gone, Sue found the dust cloth she had used the day before and set to work cleaning the last of the shelves. Not wanting to shake the dusty cloth out the front door, she stepped into the back room. The lock on the back door did stick, as Miss Ketter had said, but, by jiggling it slightly, Sue managed to open it. She shook out the cloth and closed the door, leaving it unlocked so she could open it again when she had finished the shelves.

Miss Ketter returned and the morning passed quickly. By lunchtime Sue had the remainder of the glass shelves tastefully filled in preparation for the first customer.

"May I help you with something out here?" Sue called, sticking her head into the back room.

Miss Ketter was hunched over the old desk in the corner. She stood up so quickly that her blouse sleeve caught in the pile of tissue wrapping that covered the desk and flung one loose package to the floor. It broke, releasing a flood of colored stones, earrings, bracelets and one shimmering beautiful necklace whose huge tear shaped pendant winked up at them.

"Oh, I'm sorry," Sue breathed, dropping to her knees to scoop up the treasure. "I didn't mean to startle you."

"Give those things to me." Miss Ketter's voice was harsh, her face contorted and angry. She held

9

out her hands and Sue hastily dropped the jewelry into them.

"I'm sorry," Sue repeated.

"Well, you should be," Miss Ketter snapped. "This isn't dollar-ten merchandise I'm marking." She wrapped the tissue around the lot and slid it into a drawer already nearly full of similar white packages. "You've done enough for today," she finished tartly. "Take the afternoon off." As Sue turned to leave, Miss Ketter, her voice suddenly sweet again, called after her, "Don't pay too much attention to my moods, Sue. I won't be such a grouch when we get things in order here."

Sue, fighting down the sudden tears, nodded and escaped through the front door. Five minutes later over cokes at the drugstore, Sue was telling Bruce what had happened.

"She's a terrible person to work for," Sue choked.

"Maybe it's like she says, Sue. Once she gets the shop open . . ."

"She doesn't care about the shop," Sue raged. "She didn't even bother to set up her own displays . . . let me do it instead . . . and she's a liar." She flung the last words out so loudly that old Mr. Couglin, working in the prescription department, raised his eyebrows and got ready to listen. Lowering her voice, Sue told Bruce about Miss Ketter's denying that she'd been outside the hotel the night before.

"Maybe she wasn't. You could be wrong, Sue."

10

"But I'm not," Sue cried. "If anything is wrong it's with Miss Ketter and that phony gift shop of hers."

"Going to quit?"

"Oh, Bruce," Sue shook her head, "I wish I could. Working for her will spoil my whole summer but I'll stay."

"Well, cheer up. This is the best of all possible worlds, you know," Bruce laughed. "At least, you've got the afternoon off."

When Sue stepped into the coolness of the house it seemed strangely quiet and she remembered that this was the Saturday her mother worked at the hospital. She pulled off her skirt and slipped into a pair of faded shorts. At least, she'd be able to get a tan started.

Fifteen minutes later, Sue perched on the old canvas chair in the back yard with a glass of iced tea in one hand, the morning paper in the other. News of the museum robbery filled the front page . . . Daring bandit strikes again . . . police suspect tie-up with previous burglaries . . . Idly, Sue flipped the pages searching for the rest of the story.

She found it on page five along with the photographs of the famous Crawford gem collection. Even in a news photo the necklace was lovely. Sue sat up so quickly that the glass of iced tea toppled and ran in brown rivulets down her legs. The Crawford necklace! It wasn't possible . . . possible that, this morning, with the police and private investi-

11

gators from all over the state searching for the Crawford jewels she, Sue Sterns, had been picking them up from the dusty floor of a little gift shop.

Oblivious to the mess the tea had made, Sue searched the picture again. That necklace with its same large stone . . . Could she be mistaken? She must be and still . . . If that package had held the Crawford jewels it would explain the angry way Miss Ketter had reacted. It might explain a lot of things, Sue thought as she clenched the paper in her fist and ran toward the house.

Sue had looked up the police number and lifted the receiver before finally pressing a shaky finger to cut off the connection. She had to be absolutely sure before calling Captain Wells. What she suspected to be the Crawford jewels might only be a collection of expensive costume jewelry Miss Ketter had been marking.

Thinking of the shop and Miss Ketter, Sue suddenly remembered the back door. She had forgotten to lock it again. Perhaps Miss Ketter hadn't noticed, there was no reason why she should. If the door had been left unlocked it would be the chance she needed to check . . . to see . . .

A look at the kitchen clock told Sue she still had hours to wait until it would be dark enough. Carefully, she folded the newspaper and tore out the doubt-raising picture. With trembling fingers, she placed the scrap in her blouse pocket and prepared

12

to wait for evening to come . . . for the blackness to fall that might well usher in the most dangerous night she had ever spent.

Hours later when the summer dusk had settled, Sue ducked into the alleyway behind the gift shop. She moved furtively on sneakered feet between the buildings that, except for a few lights now and then, were darkened for the night. In the daytime the narrow passageway was nothing to fear but now, in the blackness, the garbage cans and stacks of shipping boxes loomed strangely foreign in the faint moonlight and Sue found herself clutching her flashlight tighter as she peered ahead.

Once, thinking she'd heard someone following, she had nearly sprinted for the center of the alley and the safety of the street beyond but the rustling had only been the wind playing in the discarded newspapers behind the hardware store and Sue had forced herself ahead.

Seconds later she found the door to the shop and, after exploring clumsily in the dark, switched on the flashlight momentarily. The doorknob turned but the door didn't open and Sue felt her heart thud disappointingly. Miss Ketter must have noticed and locked it again. Sue tried the knob once more, this time throwing her weight against the door.

It opened, almost tumbling her into the darkened room. Sue breathed a sigh of relief. A small light burned in the front of the shop and the large window overlooked the main street. She would have to move carefully in the semi-darkness of the back room in case someone paused to survey the display in the window or one of Captain Wells' men tried the door. If she was mistaken about Miss Ketter and someone found her in the shop Sue knew she'd have no way to explain.

The newspaper clipping crackled in her pocket. Sue unfolded it and, crouching by the door leading into the shop area, studied it in the dim light. Tomorrow was Sunday. If the necklace was in the shop she had to find it tonight. Monday could be too late . . . the Crawford jewels gone.

Determinedly, Sue crossed to the back door. She pulled it tight and turned the lock as she glanced cautiously into the deserted alley. Making a shield of her hand, she switched on the flashlight and turned to the desk where she'd seen Miss Ketter put the jewelry. The drawer was locked. Her fingers explored the rest of the desk, pushing aside the papers and cartons in a frantic search for the missing key. Miss Ketter must have taken it with her. Sue was even more positive than before that the locked drawer held the secret she had suspected.

When the red glow of the flashlight glinted against the metallic outline of a pair of scissors, Sue didn't hesitate. Swiftly she wedged the tips of the scissors above the lock. At first the lock held but the surrounding wood was old and, after a min-

14

ute, it splintered and the lock gave way. Sue pulled the drawer wide, revealing the tissue wrapped packages. Quickly, thrusting the lighted flashlight into the drawer, Sue bent over it to cover the light. Her fingers were clumsy as she tore at the paper. Finally the package spilled open to reveal the jewelry she had picked up from the floor that same morning. Sue held her breath as she lifted the sparkling necklace from the pile and held it, along with the news clipping, in the circle of light. The large center diamond caught the light and prismed it back to her.

"The same. They're the same," Sue whispered.

Her hands, sorting through the rest of the packages, uncovered a curiously carved bracelet, a serpent ring and earrings that also stared back at her from the picture she held.

Triumphantly, Sue reached for the telephone just as she heard the key move in the front door lock. Perhaps it's only the on-duty policeman checking the door, Sue thought, as she peered cautiously into the store front. The light from the display window glinted into the darkness of the main street, illuminating the blondness of Miss Ketter and stippling the man beside her with light.

"The jewelry salesman!" Sue gasped.

Shrinking against the wall, she crept back toward the desk and silently lifted the phone. The operator's efficient voice made Sue glad that Bartonville hadn't yet installed the new dial telephones.

"The police. Send the police to the new gift shop . . . hurry!"

Sue's voice trailed off to a husky whisper as the front door opened and Miss Ketter and the man entered the shop. Sue slid the receiver back into its cradle and stepped into the shadows. She crouched behind a tower of cardboard cartons as the voices came nearer.

"I just don't think it's smart for us to be seen together," Miss Ketter was saying. "At least not here . . . and so often."

The man's voice was slow, confident. "So who's to know, Claire? I'm a jewelry salesman, remember? What could be more natural?"

"Well, that nosey little clerk of mine didn't seem to think it was so natural when she saw us together in the city. I think she was suspicious this morning, too."

"Well," the man accused, "it was your bright idea to hire local help, not mine."

"I don't want to have to spend all my time in this stupid shop," Miss Ketter complained. "Besides," she added confidently, "she can be controlled."

The footsteps paused as the two continued their argument. In that moment Sue glanced back at the desk and saw the open drawer and the faint glow from the flashlight that she had left burning beneath the clutter of tissue. If only she could reach the drawer, close it and get the light . . . Stealth-

16

ily, she stepped from behind the boxes. In the front room the voices rose and fell. Only a few feet . . . Sue's hand reached into the drawer. Her fingers, tightened on the flashlight, tried to still the rustle of the tissue. Her heart thumped against her ribs as she strained against the impulse to forget the light and try to reach the door she had so neatly locked, trapping herself so carelessly. She had clicked off the light and started to withdraw her hand . . . slowly . . . slowly . . .

"Working late, aren't you?"

The acid voice of Miss Ketter cut through the sudden quiet and Sue whirled to face the two. Miss Ketter switched on a light in the front room while the man pushed through the door. He pinioned Sue's arms while Miss Ketter re-entered the stock room and quickly checked the contents of the open drawer.

"She knows," Miss Ketter hissed, waving the news picture. "I told you using this shop as a front was taking a chance but oh, no, you wouldn't listen . . ."

"Be quiet," the dark man muttered. "You don't have to tell her everything."

The knocking at the front door startled them all. Suddenly Sue laughed, relief filling her voice.

"It's the police. I called them when I heard you coming."

"What can we do?"

"She couldn't have had time to tell them anything," the man said swiftly, pushing Sue forward as he spoke. "You get the door. Tell them you were working late. I'll keep an eye on her."

Forcing Sue ahead of him, he pulled her behind the wooden backed display case that angled out from the wall at the back of the store. He crouched behind her, keeping Sue's wrist in a tight grasp, so that he was hidden from view.

"If they come in here, you better watch what you say, little lady," the man growled.

He jerked his head at Miss Ketter as the knocking became a pounding. She hurried past them to open the door. Captain Wells, with Bruce right behind him, stepped through into the small shop.

"Anything wrong, ma'm? I was just on my way home when the operator called the station . . . said someone needed help here."

"Here?" Miss Ketter's voice was surprised. "Why, no. Sue and I were just working late. Getting ready for the grand opening on Monday, you know. Perhaps someone saw our lights and thought something was wrong."

"Then neither of you called for help?" Captain Wells asked, turning to look at Sue.

Sue felt the pressure of the man's fingers against her wrist as she spoke. "Why, no, Captain Wells." She stared at Bruce and tried to smile as she spoke. "The only trouble we're having is getting the shop ready in time for the opening. Outside of that, this is the best of all possible worlds."

For a second, Sue thought that Bruce understood but when Captain Wells turned toward the door Bruce followed his father.

"Well, if everything's all right we'll let you two ladies get back to work. Success in your new business," the captain smiled as they backed into the street, closing the door behind them.

Sue felt the tears sting her lids as Miss Ketter latched the door behind the Wells and hurried back to where the man held Sue. He stood up then and prodded Sue into the back room.

"Grab that stuff," he muttered, pointing to the packages. "I'll tie Miss Nosey up and by the time they find her we'll be long gone."

"Some idea," Miss Ketter snapped as she scooped up the jewelry. "Spending a thousand dollars to set up this phony shop and getting caught before we even open."

"Well, it worked for us before," the man grunted sarcastically, "and it would have again except for her." He nodded at Sue as he bound her to the straight backed desk chair. "One good thing," he laughed shortly, "we haven't paid for most of the merchandise yet and with these," he jammed one of the tissue bundles into his pocket, "with these we should be pretty well set for awhile."

He finished speaking and, while Miss Ketter dropped the last of the Crawford jewels into a paper sack, he turned back to Sue.

"Sorry, little lady, but this is what you get for being so inquisitive."

The handkerchief cut into Sue's mouth as he pulled it tight and knotted it behind her head. Sue watched in dismay as Miss Ketter switched out the lights, leaving the shop and the small back room in total darkness.

"We'd better use the back door," Miss Ketter said. "In case that policeman is still hanging around."

Sue heard the back door lock click open and then, in the pale light from the distant street lights, watched the two thieves step into the alley. She was trying to free herself from the cord that bound her when she heard the crash of falling garbage cans and the clear, strong voice of Captain Wells.

"I thought Bruce was crazy," the captain said later as they untied Sue, "but he was so positive that something was wrong that we decided to check."

"A good thing we did, too," Bruce smiled. "The Marshes . . . that's your Miss Ketter and her husband . . . had worked this same routine on the east coast a few years ago. She sets up a small shop and then, acting as a salesman, he delivers the things he's stolen."

"And when things cool down a little," Bruce's father continued, "they reach their contacts who come to buy the jewelry and smaller items right from the shop."

20

"Well," Sue said ruefully, "I've probably done myself right out of a summer job . . ."

"There's probably a reward," Captain Wells grinned.

"Even if there isn't," Sue said, "tonight has taught me one thing . . . Bartonville has the best of all possible police captains." She giggled as she saw Bruce and his father exchange glances. "This time I really mean it," Sue added with a smile, "and I'll even add that the best of all possible captains has the smartest of all possible sons."

Summer Office Girl

EVELYN DORIO

JILL Trenton jumped up from the patio lounge chair and blew a kiss toward her uncle. "Thank you, Uncle Philip. Thank you for giving me a chance. And I hope you'll be proud of me as your summer office girl."

"Glad to help my ambitious niece," he replied. He was finishing the sandwich and glass of iced tea which Jill had prepared for him when he came by to discuss their plans.

"And Uncle Philip," continued Jill, "will you promise me something? Please don't tell anyone in your office that I'm your niece. Let's keep that a secret. I want to make the grade on my own. I don't want any special favors!" Ever since Jill had learned about the office position with the U.S. Operation Mission Overseas, she was determined to prove to her parents that she was competent and capable enough to be allowed to go to Spain. How exciting it would be to work in the U.S. Embassy in Madrid! Three months in her uncle's architectural office would be her opportunity now to prove herself. "When do I begin, Uncle Philip?"

"Monday morning. I'll call for you at about 7:15. I'll let you off three blocks from the office, to make sure nobody sees us coming to work together. How's that? Then, in the evening, I'll pick you up at the same place and drive you home. I'll pretend you're the daughter of a . . . a college fraternity brother who made unfortunate investments. And you have to work to support yourself. OK?"

"That's a perfect secret!" Jill laughed.

"Speaking of secrets," her uncle's voice went low, "there's something I must explain about our work; something strictly confidential. Even your parents don't know about this. Some of the work in my office has to do with secret government contracts. The work is part of our national defense— that's all I can tell you about it. These jobs are done in a separate drafting room—we call it the Dead End because of its location."

"Uncle Philip! I never knew you did secret work!"

"Of course, only authorized personnel have access to that room," her uncle continued, "but you'll be in the office, and there's always the chance that you'll hear bits of information. No matter how careful the men are, it's possible for information to leak out. Be careful, Jill, when you're talking to other people, to your friends. Never reveal anything about my office to anyone, never so much as a word. You understand?"

"I'm glad you trust me enough to tell me this," said Jill. "And I'll work hard to deserve that confidence."

"It's an honor to be entrusted with such contracts. Right now we're working on a secret project which we call *Montecello*. It's so vital to our country that even our drawing scraps are kept track of—they're numbered and checked and then burned in the incinerator after work—always in the presence of an army engineer. If any information about *Montecello* leaked out to the enemies of the free world, not only would all my government contracts be cancelled, but our country would be endangered."

"I'll remember that, Uncle Philip."

"We have a guard at the door during working hours. His name is Mac, but the men call him The Dragon. If it's necessary for him to leave his post, even for a moment, he locks the door to Dead End. I'm telling you this, Jill, so you'll realize how important secrecy is. The enemy is ruthless and just as determined to pry out our secrets as we're determined to keep them from doing it. So, be alert, Jill. Be observant. And if you ever see any-

25

thing, or hear anything that doesn't seem quite right to you, let me know. And fast!"

"It takes my breath away! But it'll be wonderful training for working in the U.S. Embassy in Spain, won't it?"

"Exactly the kind of training you need."

Early Monday morning Jill's uncle picked her up at the curb and soon his car was rolling through freeway traffic toward La Ventura. After they had come through the interchange, Jill got off and walked the last three blocks to the Verdon architectural offices.

A neatly-dressed woman in a black suit set off with gold jewelry greeted Jill. "I'm Gladys Bellman," she said. "I'm Mr. Verdon's secretary. He told me about you." Her brown eyes were warm and friendly, and the thread of gray in her black hair increased her attractiveness. "Your desk is next to mine, Jill, in the reception room," Gladys continued. "I'll explain your work through the day. Anything you don't understand . . . just ask me. First, we'll open the mail. When we deliver it to the different section heads, I'll introduce you."

As Jill began to slit envelopes, the office came to life. The switchboard buzzed, voices sounded over the intercom; the postman waited to have a receipt signed, two clients, trim and polished, arrived for early appointments, a salesman holding a stuffed sample case waited patiently. From the main drafting room, Jill heard wheels rolling over tile floors, cabinet doors banging and men's voices in snatches of baseball talk. So this is what an architectural office is like! she thought. This is where important work is done—shopping centers, office buildings, banks. Even secret government work.

In a few minutes Kay Simpson, switchboard operator, arrived. She was younger than Gladys, livelier and more glamorous, perhaps, in a green striped silk dress and narrow-heeled pumps. Her auburn hair was arranged in a stylish bouffant.

"You're late again," said Gladys. "I've already taken three calls—one from that impatient Mr. Weilhard from army engineers. Why aren't you able to get here on time?"

Kay's lashes flickered as she walked, twirling her car keys, toward the lounge.

"Come with me, Jill," said Gladys. She lifted the pile of opened mail. "We'll make the rounds together."

In the main drafting room, Jill saw fifteen or twenty desks, arranged in rows of three, with high backless stools on which draftsmen sat. Water color drawings, dull-tinted T-squares and pink lucite triangles cluttered the drawing boards. Scattered on a dozen tables were rolls of tracing paper, magazines and colored pencils. An entire wall was studded with tubes containing blueprints of completed jobs.

"Gentlemen," said Gladys, "this is Jill Trenton, our summer office girl. She's just starting in this morning. Jill, these men design only the most beautiful buildings in La Ventura."

"All between coffee breaks, too," quipped a clean-cut man of about thirty-five whose broad smile seemed as pleasant as his voice. "Hello, Jill. I'm Eric Colyer."

Next Jill met Mr. Role and Mr. Brunetti in the front row; then she lost track of the names Gladys called off. Next Gladys led Jill to a small table on which were an electric plate, piles of cups and a can of coffee. "This corner is the Cafe de Paris. It's your job to make the coffee, Jill, and," she laughed, "the first thing you'll learn is that no two people in this office like it the same strength."

As they passed the water cooler Gladys said, "And this is the Gossip Well. You can find out everything that happens in this office just by standing here. You can even find out things that never happen!" Behind the cooler was tacked a small sign which read: DON'T SNILE—SMARL.

Next Gladys showed Jill the lounge. Kay, standing in front of a mirror, was spraying her hair.

"Mr. Verdon's expecting an important call from Fresmonds," said Gladys. "You should be at your board."

Kay snapped down the top of the spray can, and Gladys and Jill returned to the hallway.

Dead End was guarded, as Jill's uncle had told her, by Mac. His blue uniform fit snugly over muscular shoulders; wrinkles made distinct patterns over his stern face. "You and I can't enter this room," said Gladys, "but let's just peek in for a moment."

"Make it swift," said Mac.

Several men, holding rolled-up drawings, were talking earnestly in the secret room. They acknowledged Jill's presence with a brief nod and resumed their conference. Then Gladys showed Jill the reference library, piled with technical magazines and books, and the brightly-lit sample room that seemed a helter-skelter of paint charts and slabs of tile and wood. Back in the hall, Gladys pointed out the Japanese ash door which led to Mr. Verdon's private office.

"Well, that's it," said Gladys, as they returned to the reception room. "You've met everyone except Ned Wright. He comes in at two o'clock. He attends the SC School of Architecture, part-time, and works here three or four hours in the afternoon."

The morning passed swiftly. Jill learned to use the postage meter and the mimeograph, walked to the post office to register a letter and delivered a drawing to a client. She enjoyed every task.

After lunch Gladys showed Jill how to run the print machine. Running off prints from tracings would be Jill's main job. First she learned to make developing fluid and then she watched the tracing revolve on the big roller on its way to the liquid bath. Black ducts overhead drew off the fumes. At first the enormous block-like machine seemed complicated, but after four or five trials, Jill understood the process so well that she set the machine at higher speed. It would be her responsibility to turn on the machine in the morning and switch it off again at closing time.

Jill was busily running off prints for Mr. Role when Ned arrived. He had the college boy's lanky look, a dark crewcut and finely-cut features. While driving the freeway this morning, Jill's uncle had referred to Ned as "promising material."

The afternoon coffee break brought almost the whole staff, even the Dead Enders, to the Cafe de Paris. Jill thought this was the most fun of the day. There was a great rush for coffee and cupcakes. The room seemed about to explode with the shouts and banter of twenty or thirty men. Jill only wished she could understand more of the shop-talk.

She was nibbling the cupcake icing when Eric came over for a re-fill. He had spent a number of years in Europe on a Beaux Arts scholarship, and when Jill told him she hoped to go to Spain in September he exclaimed, "Ah! I shall have to tell you about Spain! Actually, most of the country is run-down, poor; but Madrid is delightful! What fun I've had in those cafes! You know, the Spaniards are the most handsome people in all of Europe. To-morrow I'll bring you some folders on Madrid."

Jill was washing cups when she noticed Gladys beside her. "Coffee?" asked Jill.

"No, thank you. Jill, don't leave the reception room too long at coffee break. I mean, in the future . . ."

Jill nodded, though she doubted she could make coffee, pour it and wash cups in less time than she had taken.

As soon as Gladys left, Kay came in. "Any coffee? Oh! That woman gets under my skin!"

"Like a cupcake?" asked Jill. "There're three or four left."

"Not for my figure." Kay smoothed her skirt carefully. "I've got a date tonight. That's why I'm gussied up. Dinner at Figaro's on the Sunset Strip —with Eric. When Gladys finds out, her gold necklace'll tarnish green!"

Mr. Brunetti came alongside, handed Jill several tracings and said he needed ten copies of each. They would be sent to contractors for bids. Could she start right away? By the time she finished, the draftsmen were cleaning up desks and floor and stuffing paper scraps into enormous wastebaskets. From down the hall she heard Mac locking the door to Dead End.

It's been a wonderful day, Jill thought, as she waited for her uncle at their appointed place. Exciting, too, even though I didn't meet a single enemy agent trying to pry out secret information from me!

As weeks passed, Jill gained in experience and confidence. I have to make good, she reminded herself. I must prove to my parents that I'm capable of looking after myself. This experience of living and working abroad—it means so much to me. I want to understand more about people.

Ned Wright became her closest office friend. They spent many Saturday afternoons visiting Barnsdall Park and modern art galleries off Wilshire Boulevard, or attending lectures at Hancock Auditorium. Ned's father was killed at Tarawa in World War II, and Ned had to work for his education. Jill sometimes wondered what lay beyond his years of study. Her uncle always gave Ned great encouragement in his work.

One afternoon in early September, Jill was busy running prints for Mr. Brunetti until 5:30. The day had been hectic—a continually buzzing switchboard, clients hurrying in and out, typewriters and mimeograph going all afternoon. No one lingered at the Cafe de Paris. The Dead Enders hadn't even stopped for a coffee break. As Jill walked the three blocks to meet her uncle, she realized she had forgotten several parcels she'd bought during her lunch hour. They contained buttons and zippers she intended to use on dresses she was sewing for her trip to Spain. Though she disliked keeping her uncle waiting, especially after such a busy day, she hurried back to the office for her packages.

Since Jill knew the front door would be locked,

she came through the rear parking lot. Mac and Mr. Weilhard were standing in front of the double-chambered incinerator and burning the scraps from Dead End. Mr. Weilhard, a loosely-jointed and stalwart blond, examined each scrap sheet and checked its number before crumpling it into the flames. The secret project, *Montecello,* Jill remembered, had been finished today.

Jill hurried to the lounge, but when she didn't find her parcels there, she decided she must have left them in her desk. As she passed the drafting room, Eric spoke to her, but she didn't understand him and walked toward his desk to hear better. He was intently examining a drawing on his board, but turned to her as she approached. "Cigarette?" he asked. He blew smoke away from his board.

"Now, Eric, you know I don't smoke."

She decided to check the print machine and noticed that the light was on. "I thought . . . Eric, didn't I turn off the light when I left the office?" she asked.

"It's been a day of confusion all around," said Eric.

"You like cup coffee?" asked Mr. Brunetti from the Cafe de Paris. He had just finished pouring a cup of black liquid for himself.

"Thank you, but that special brew of yours . . ."

"Italian coffee," said Mr. Brunetti, "is . . . a challenge."

"I get the feeling it might corrode my stomach."

33

"Corrode?" repeated Mr. Brunetti and then joined her laughter.

Jill caught a quick smile from Ned and a moment later entered the reception room. She pulled up short. Gladys was kneeling on the floor beside a pile of wastebasket scraps. She jumped up when Jill entered and walked to her desk without speaking. After Jill recovered from her surprise, she found the parcels in the lower drawer of her desk and hurried back to meet her uncle. He made the half-turn to the on ramp and, after a few tense moments of checking side-view mirror and slowing and accelerating the motor by turn, he joined the traffic stream.

Jill kept thinking of what she had seen: Gladys going through the wastebasket scraps . . . Maybe it wasn't important. Maybe she'd lost something. Still, it seemed strange, and she'd offered no explanation. "Uncle Philip," Jill began, "remember when I first started to work how you cautioned me . . . You said to be alert, be observant. And that if anything didn't seem . . ."

"What's up?" he interrupted.

"When I returned to the office just now, Gladys . . ."

"Gladys? She left at five o'clock!"

"I know. I saw her. But when I went back just now, the wastebasket trash had been emptied on the floor and Gladys seemed to be going through it.

34

In one pile the scraps were all crumpled and in the other, they'd been smoothed out as though . . ."

"Are you sure?" His grip tightened on the wheel. "In other offices scraps are scraps. But in ours . . . If by any mistake, one of the men . . . An enemy could learn a lot from our scraps. I'll phone Mac soon as I get home. No, I'll take the next off ramp and drive back to the office."

"I wonder what Gladys was looking for," said Jill, but her uncle didn't answer.

He parked in the rear lot and tried the door. It was locked. The sooty smell of recent burning lingered in the air, but all cars had gone from the parking area.

Next morning Jill was barely at her desk when the switchboard buzzed. Gladys, answering, called, "Mr. Verdon! Mr. Weilhard calling. Urgent! Urgent!" Her hands pulled nervously at her throat as she returned to her desk.

A few seconds later Jill heard her uncle's voice over the intercom, "Everyone go to the main drafting room! At once! Main drafting room!"

Shushing voices, drawers hastily slammed, stools dragged across the floor, rushing footsteps . . .

"What's wrong?" Jill whispered to Eric.

"We probably drew the medical center plans without a floor. Or maybe without a roof."

"Eric, don't be facetious at a time like this!" reprimanded Gladys. "This sounds serious!"

Jill's uncle entered, his face ashen-gray. "I've just had a call from Weilhard, Army Engineers. Last night the FBI found a set of prints of our secret project, *Montecello,* in the possession of an enemy agent."

Silence; then the let-go of bated breath; tumble of questioning voices. Stunned silence again.

"Maybe is mistake?" said Mr. Brunetti as he lit a cigarette.

"The FBI doesn't make mistakes," replied Uncle Philip. Color returned slowly to his cheeks. "No one is to leave this room until Mr. Mortenson arrives. He's from the FBI office."

Gladys leaned against a stool and turned her face sharply away.

Jill looked at each employee by turn. Was it possible? One person among them was a traitor, an enemy agent. Which one? A sickening feeling registered in the pit of her stomach. Which one was the traitor? The thing her uncle feared, had happened. The enemy of the free world . . . Secret plans . . . Suddenly she realized her own precarious position. I was here after working hours! she remembered. If only I hadn't returned for my parcels! Now I'm involved. Will anyone believe my motive for returning? Will I have to prove my innocence? Fine way to convince my parents that I'm able to manage my affairs! And Gladys . . . She was here, too. I wonder what she was searching for.

Mr. Mortenson was slender and middle-aged, with a disarming manner. "I'll try not to disrupt your office routine any more than necessary," he began. "I'd like to make a rundown of all employees who were in the office yesterday and what time each one left."

He turned to Gladys. "Bring me the employees' application card file, please."

He attacked his job of questioning with relish. Soon he released most of the staff, but asked Ned, Eric, Mr. Brunetti, Gladys and Jill—all who had been in the office late—to meet in Mr. Verdon's private office.

"Miss Trenton, I'll begin with you." Sharp blue eyes focused on Jill. "Explain step by step what you did when you returned to the office last night."

Jill prayed for courage. Thoughtfully she related her movements from her entry to hearing Eric speak. "The print machine light was on, and I turned it off."

"Don't you always switch off the print machine at night?" asked Mr. Mortenson.

"Yes, that's my responsibility. And I thought I *had*."

"Continue," said Mr. Mortenson.

"I went past what we call the Cafe de Paris. Mr. Brunetti asked whether I'd like some coffee. Then I went into the reception room."

"Mr. Mortenson," said her uncle. Jill shook her head vigorously, and her lips formed "NO!" If she

37

was under suspicion, she'd clear herself! She didn't want him to become implicated on her account!

"Miss Trenton," Mr. Mortenson's voice was polite and detached, "you worked until 5:30. Do you think that in your hurry to leave you may have forgotten to turn off the print machine?"

"It's possible, but not likely," said Jill firmly. "I really believe . . . I turned it off."

"Then why did you check it? You can't even see the light from Eric's desk."

That was true.

"Why did you check the machine?"

"I don't . . . really know."

"*Montecello* was completed at four o'clock yesterday," continued Mr. Mortenson. "The confiscated prints must have been made between that time and 6:05, the time the men in the drafting room locked the rear door of the office and went home."

Jill caught a dark look from Mr. Brunetti.

Then Mr. Mortenson asked, "Eric, was Miss Trenton in the drafting room long enough to run off a print?"

Eric's face jerked in surprise. "Maybe if the machine was already warmed up—it has to be warmed up, you know. Maybe . . ."

"Did she run off a print?"

"I can't say that she did or that she didn't. All I know is what I was doing—working at my own desk."

38

Mr. Mortenson picked up the box of employee cards. "Either Miss Trenton didn't turn off the machine after work last night, or someone turned it back on after she left and made the prints of the secret project. It takes three or four minutes for the machine to warm up. Once it's turned off, it can't be turned on again for ten minutes. Since the time element in this matter is so important, I'm pointing out these facts."

I must have turned it off, thought Jill. I must have. It's become automatic, after doing it all these weeks. But I did leave in a hurry, and there's always the possibility . . . Such a hectic day . . . I wish I could remember exactly, exactly.

"I'd like to continue," said Mr. Mortenson. "Miss Trenton, you say that Eric was at his drawing board, is that right?"

"Yes. I remember he offered me a cigarette. He was blowing smoke away from his board as I approached."

"Please, I go now?" asked Mr. Brunetti. "Mr. Fresmond wait for his drawing. Mr. Fresmond . . . hurry-hurry!" Mr. Brunetti waved his hands over his head.

Mr. Mortenson selected Mr. Brunetti's card from the file. "You're Italian-born?"

"I was born een Tunisia. My father was army officer there."

"Where did you live in Italy?"

"I never live in Italy. I come directly to America."

"Return to your board, Mr. Brunetti. I'll call you later."

Mr. Mortenson then asked Ned what he was doing in the office last night.

"I'll answer that," said Eric. "He was changing a detail on the Fresmond job—they didn't like the way the door swung in the entry."

Mr. Mortenson read Eric's card next: "Lived in La Ventura five years; California state architectural license."

"Eric is my finest designer," said Jill's uncle. "I appreciate a man for whom architecture is an art as well as a job."

"Married?" queried Mr. Mortenson.

"My fiancée was killed in an airplane accident five years ago. She was flying to California to meet me. We were to be married."

Jill glanced up. She'd often wondered about Eric, so attractive, well-read, traveled. Now she remembered his sudden mood changes—probably he still mourned that girl's death.

When Gladys' turn came she began, "I may as well tell you, Mr. Mortenson. I was going through the wastebasket scraps. Jill saw me. But it had nothing to do with *Montecello!* You'll have to believe me!"

"What were you looking for?" Mr. Mortenson asked unemotionally.

Gladys covered her face with her hands.

"Return to your desk, Miss Bellman." Mr. Mortenson's voice was gentle. "I'll talk to you later."

Jill's uneasiness mounted as Mr. Mortenson turned again to her. "Miss Trenton, you've said that you checked the print machine and the coffee corner—the very things which are your responsibility to check each night before you leave, isn't that so?"

Jill realized that suspicion pointed to her. She ran most of the prints; she turned on the machine, turned it off. She couldn't shake off the feeling that she'd been negligent. She'd failed her uncle. Fine chance I have of being allowed to go to Spain, she thought, when this happens right in my uncle's office! Would the government cancel his contracts now? And even though the FBI had caught those prints in time, how much had the enemy already learned? What danger . . . ? and maybe all through her own negligence.

Later, when Jill was metering the mail, Mr. Mortenson called her into her uncle's office. "Miss Trenton, Mr. Verdon has just explained your relationship. Now I can confide something: the *Montecello* plans we confiscated were not prints made by your machine. They were photographs, four sectional views taken by a camera."

"But you said . . ."

"I pursued that line of questioning hoping to bring out something we don't know."

41

Jill sat down. "Then you didn't really suspect me? At least, on that point, I feel relieved."

"Now we've got to find out how the enemy agent took those photographs and," his words slowed, "who the enemy agent is."

"But I would have seen a camera!" exclaimed Jill. "Anyone would!"

"Jill, it's possible to have a camera small enough to fit into the palm of one's hand. Think back on the whole day. Visualize the entire office scene when you returned for your parcels. Somewhere in your mind may be registered the very clue we need. You may go, now."

After work Jill met her uncle at the customary corner. He made the short turn to the on ramp and joined the flow of freeway traffic.

"Uncle Philip, your turn signal is still clicking," Jill reminded him.

"Thanks, Jill. The wheels don't make a complete turn at that spot. Corner isn't sharp enough."

The sound of the clicking turn signal lingered in Jill's mind, then faded from her consciousness as she glanced over the kaleidoscope of city life: church towers ghostly through bluish haze, rock-roofed housing projects, white clothes fluttering, treetops, like spires into the sky . . . Suddenly she heard in her mind the clicking turn signal again. The clicking reminded her of another pattern. What was it? A rainbird sprinkler when the water pressure was coming up . . . The aluminum kettle ticked like that when Mr. Brunetti absentmindedly boiled away his coffee-water. The print machine ticked that way, if it cooled off too rapidly. Suddenly she sat up. *Click, click, click, click.* She heard it clearly. But where? Not a sprinkler head. Not her uncle's turn signal, not the aluminum kettle, not the print machine. Distinctly, four times, with only slight breaks between, she was hearing it again. She imagined herself walking down the hall, past the drafting room. *Click, click, click, click.* Could that be? *Somewhere in your mind may be registered the very clue we need. The very clue!* That was why I checked the print machine! And the coffee corner! I was trying to trace that sound! "Uncle Philip! Oh, Uncle Philip! I wonder if . . . ?"

Mr. Mortenson was still in the office when Jill and her uncle rushed breathlessly in. Within minutes Jill was reconstructing last night's scene when she had returned for her parcels. "Just as I passed the drafting room," she tried to restrain the tumbling of her words, "Eric spoke to me, yes, but it was another sound that caught my mind. It was the clicking. And it's true, Eric was smoking, and the small object in his hand did click like a lighter. But it was not a lighter. *Not a lighter!* And what seemed to be a natural motion of blowing smoke away was really a naturally protective gesture over his drawing board."

43

"I still can't believe it, Jill," said her uncle. "I've trusted Eric . . ."

"That was a camera in the palm of his hand," said Mr. Mortenson.

"And the clicking I heard," continued Jill, "made the four pictures which the FBI confiscated. That was why I checked the print machine and the coffee corner—I was subconsciously trying to explain that sound."

"This is Eric's ashtray." Mr. Mortenson picked up an attractively decorated pottery bowl. "Look! It's filled with burned ends of matches. Eric doesn't even use a lighter."

"My most talented designer! I can't believe it! Whatever possessed him? Why would a man who has everything turn traitor to his own country?"

Mr. Mortenson went into Uncle Philip's private office to make a phone call. When he returned he said, "Eric must have lacked something, probably money, a lot of money, the kind he needs in order to live high—trips to Europe, fine hotels, gourmet restaurants. But there must have been psychological reasons, too—strong hatred, a need to get even about something."

"Maybe the death of his fiancée," suggested Jill.

"Maybe."

"But how did Eric manage to get the drawing?" asked her uncle. "It was in Dead End. Don't tell me Mac's in on this! Nobody, but nobody's allowed in there except authorized personnel!"

"Oh, no, Mac's not involved," replied Mr. Mortenson, "not that old dragon! But the only way I can see . . . it's possible that Eric had a key made, maybe when he first started to work for you. You liked him, trusted him. There'd be no reason for you to suspect him."

"I admired his ability."

"He probably worked late, sometimes, didn't he?"

"Of course. All the men do, if they have to finish a certain job."

"That's when he had his chance."

"But how did he do it? I mean, the photographs."

"I can only tell you what I think," said Mr. Mortenson. "Yesterday, when the project was finished and Mac and Weilhard were burning the scraps, Eric knew he had to hurry and do his job before the work was mailed out. He could easily have let himself into Dead End, got the plans, placed them on his own drawing board—a most natural place —and proceeded to take his pictures. Ned and Mr. Brunetti were busy with their own work. Then Eric must have returned the drawing before Mac came back from the scrap burning. Only slip-up in Eric's plans was Jill's unexpected appearance—at a most crucial moment!"

"And I never dreamed, Mr. Mortenson . . . I never . . ."

"Of course, you didn't."

"But what about Gladys?" asked Jill. "Did she have any part in it?"

Mr. Mortenson shook his head. "Gladys is in love with Eric, has been for a long time. Apparently everything was going along fine with them—or so she thought—until he began to date Kay. Probably the only reason Eric dated either of them was to get information about your secret work."

Jill noticed her uncle shaking his head in disbelief.

"Yesterday afternoon Eric wrote Kay a note," continued Mr. Mortenson, "no doubt about their date plans, and Gladys returned to the office to hunt for it among the wastebasket scraps. That was all."

Uncle Philip was still slumped in his chair. "I'm glad your men confiscated the pictures, Mr. Mortenson. I'm really glad! I don't even want to think . . . what might have happened. But I suppose . . . I suppose my government contracts will be cancelled, now."

The phone rang, and Mr. Mortenson took the call in the private office. Satisfaction glinted in his eyes when he returned a few moments later. "Eric Colyer's been taken into custody. Seems he was leaving on a trip—to Europe. All packed, ready to go. Well, this is one trip he won't make . . . About those government contracts, Mr. Verdon. I understand your feelings. But there's another way to look at it. Wait till Central Intelligence hears Eric is the

46

man we've been trying to track down these last four or five years!"

"You mean you were looking for him?"

"We were looking for a very slick agent . . . someone who managed somehow to get vital information into enemy hands. Let's just say you saved Eric for us!"

"Mr. Mortenson," said Jill, "what's going to happen to Eric?"

Mr. Mortenson took her arm. "Jill, every agent knows his occupational hazards. If he gets caught, that's it! The country which employed him won't even acknowledge him. It's part of the job. Eric knew that at the start."

After a moment's reflection Jill said, "There's still something I'd like to know. Did I really forget to turn off the print machine last night, or did someone turn it on after I left the office?"

Mr. Mortenson sat back in his chair and smiled. "What a time I had digging out that bit of information! You turned it off, Jill. You did it automatically. But Mr. Brunetti turned it on. He needed several more prints on the Fresmond job, and since you'd left the office, he went ahead and made them himself. Nothing wrong with that. But all the time we were talking about the light; the light, he thought we meant the electric light. And since he hadn't turned on any electric light—the office lights had been on all day—he couldn't figure out . . . It was only after I made him repeat every action that I realized we weren't talking about the same light."

Later when Jill's uncle had made the on-ramp turn to the freeway she said, "Uncle Philip, your turn signal is still clicking."

"Good girl," he laughed. "Never can remember. But I was just thinking, Jill . . . I'm proud of you, my summer office girl. I feel as though you've proved . . . you've more than proved you can look after yourself, no matter where you are. I think your parents are going to allow you . . ."

Jill wasn't listening. She wondered whether Ned's letters to her in Madrid would be long, real long.

Nightmare Party

————◆————◆————◆————◆————

PEG GRANGER

TRACY Roberts slumped in the corner of the back seat, glumly looking out at the rows and rows of tract houses streaking by the car window. Ridiculous, the whole situation was! Ironic, too. Here she had been practically forced by her mother to come to the city to spend the summer with her cousin and what is the first thing they do? Pile into a car with a bunch of stuck-up city kids and head out to the country! Judy is nice enough, Tracy reasoned, and I like her. But to be marooned with these snobbish kids? And for what? Tracy slumped down even farther. A mysterious houseparty! Only mysterious thing about it I can see, Tracy thought grumpily, is that I'm going at all!

She ran her fingers over her tousled brown hair, her eyebrows furrowed over her blue eyes. She plucked a tiny speck of fuzz off her brand new capri pants and tried to concentrate on the landscape outside. There were fewer houses now and occasionally Tracy could get a glimpse between billboards of what they doubtless called "country" around here. The lowering southern California sun slanted on a checkerboard of flat farmland, stretching on as far as she could see. Tracy thought longingly of the hills back home at Crowley's Corners in northern California. Her country was not like this! Her country was shimmering mounds of emerald grass that seemed to change color like watered silk whenever the wind blew. She sighed. She wouldn't see any of it again until the grass had turned yellow, then changed to twisted stalks in the cold of autumn.

"Why the sigh, Tracy? Worried about the mystery?" Jeep Hendricks asked from the front seat. Tracy scowled at the back of his head. One thing she was definitely not worried about was this mystery they all kept babbling about.

"Not really," she answered. Some mystery it will probably be anyway, she thought. Probably a wildly dangerous game of tiddlywinks in the dark, or something. She stared out the window. That Jeep Hendricks hadn't helped matters, either. He was one of the nicest-looking boys she had ever seen, and just the type she liked with sandy, close-cropped hair and intense blue eyes. But he had this same offhand who-are-you kind of attitude the rest of them had. Oh, if only she could go home where she knew everyone and people acted like people instead of bit players in a high budget movie!

"Wait till you see the Andrews' place!" Judy exclaimed from the front seat. "They raise blooded stock and it's so perfect and picturesque it hardly looks real. Everything, absolutely everything, is whitewashed till it hurts your eyes to look at it—"

"Even the grass?" Tracy asked disagreeably.

Mary Hendricks glanced over at her, her eyebrows raised. Tracy looked back and her heart sank. Jeep's sister was typical of the whole crowd. She looked—well, right. Her blonde hair hung straight and shining to her shoulders and her lipstick was the exact shade of her casual Bermuda shorts. She looked as if she would fit in wherever she was, even here in the back seat where she was looking at Tracy as if she were a specimen on a slide.

Finally Jeep turned off the highway onto a white dirt road slicing through a pasture so green it looked touched up with vegetable dye. On a slight rise ahead Tracy could see a huge, gabled house with several rambling outbuildings around it. Judy hadn't exaggerated. It looked like a picture book farmhouse, a study in green and white outlined against the sky. There was even a little old Dutch-style windmill in the middle of the pasture to her left. Riotous splotches of flower beds were everywhere.

"I'll bet it isn't real," Tracy said, half to herself. "Probably made out of cardboard just to complete the picture."

"What?" Judy asked.

"Oh. I meant the windmill over there."

"It works," Jeep said. "Can't you see the blades going around?"

Sure I can, Tracy thought. And I can also see that there isn't a breath of wind. These city-bred kids didn't even know that nobody used windmills anymore. No doubt this Mr. Andrews had a neat little electric motor to make his windmill look official while modern pumping equipment did all the work. And he probably stalked around in blue jeans while hired hands really ran the place! How different, she thought, staring at the beautiful horses in the pasture as they sped by, how very different from the honest, working farm, back home.

They came to a stop outside a shaded veranda— nothing that big could possibly be called a porch. A group of young people and a handsome, middle-aged couple walked down the flagstone steps to meet them. Tracy glanced down at her glaringly new outfit in dismay. Everyone else had on blue jeans and huge, shapeless sweatshirts. She nodded to them all, frozen-faced, as Judy introduced her.

"Just in time to go to your rooms and freshen up a bit before dinner," Mr. Andrews said. "We're barbecuing steaks out by the pool." His smile widened. "Everybody all set for mystery?"

The young people all smiled and nodded and trailed into the big house. Two maids showed them their rooms, arranged along a huge, high-raftered hall at the top of the biggest curving staircase Tracy had ever seen outside the movies.

Later, as she and Judy went down the stairs to join the others for dinner, Judy said, "This is an annual thing, you know. The Andrews have given this weekend party ever since we were all in seventh grade. And each year after dinner Mr. Andrews has this fabulous game—"

I knew it, Tracy thought sourly.

"Well, I'll let him explain it," Judy went on as they joined the others. "But it's lots of fun."

The dinner was as unbelievably perfect as everything else. The brick terrace at the side of the house overlooked a pool that would have been called a lake anywhere else. Tracy sat miserably on the edge of a white-upholstered chair and poked at her dinner.

"Where did you say you were from?" Sue Andrews asked.

"Me?" Tracy asked stupidly. Well, who else! she thought in disgust. The rest of these kids have known each other since seventh grade! She looked at the faces, white blobs staring curiously under the dancing lights of the Tiki torches all around the terrace. Tell them about Crowley's Corners? It would be like exposing something precious. Her country wasn't the Andrews' country! "Uh—just out of San Francisco," she answered. She ignored Judy's quick glance. Crowley's Corners was about as close to San Francisco as it was to the moon!

"Really?" Sue said. "Where did you go to school?"

"Uh—" She was saved by the hearty voice of Bart Andrews.

"Well, come on, everybody. Let's go into the den. I have a tremendous mystery game for you this time!" Maids silently drifted in among the tables removing the dinner plates as the group followed Mr. Andrews into the house.

"Sure you were finished?" Jeep asked, standing next to Tracy and observing her barely-touched plate.

"I wasn't very hungry," she answered and went into the house with him. She perched on the arm of a couch that looked about forty feet long.

"Here's how it will go," Mr. Andrews was saying. "This year all the action will take place outside. There's a prize—and this time I think I've outdone myself on the prize! But it's going to be hard to win. What you have to do is follow the clues I've left around. They're subtle and they're hard to find and you're going to have to work in the dark. The moon will be up later, but there will be no help from lighting sources besides the torches outside. You're to work in pairs. Keep your wits about you and stay close to your partner. It will probably take you a couple of hours."

"What if it doesn't, Mr. Andrews?" one of the boys spoke up. "What if we find the—er—prize ahead of time?"

"Then come and tell me," he said, "I'll be just inside the sliding doors in here, and I'll blow this whistle to bring you all in. Oh, yes. The areas where the clues are distributed are in the patio, pool decking, tennis courts and the two small pastures out by the drive. Okay?"

"Okay," they chorused and all headed for the patio. Jeep picked up Tracy's limp hand.

"Come on," he said somewhat grimly. "Let's go do the best we can. This prize is liable to really be something. Last year it was a stereo hi-fi set and he apologized about it."

What show-offs, Tracy thought as she stumbled after Jeep. Some mystery! She bet it wouldn't be as much fun as the scavenger hunts back home.

The flickering light of the Tiki torches cast weird shadows in the shrubbery and trees alongside the patio. Tracy felt a shiver run up her spine in spite of herself. The couples spread out and their excited cries were quickly swallowed up in the darkness that seemed to wait outside the shimmering circlets of light. They were the only two left. Jeep left her side and was prowling around the white furniture, picking up cushions and looking under tables. Uncertain what to do Tracy ventured beyond the lighted area. When her eyes got accustomed to the dark she spotted a strange greenish glow almost hidden under a huge flowering bush.

"Jeep?" she quavered. "I think I've found something." He was right at her side.

"Where?"

"Under there. It—it sort of glows." He reached under and pulled out a piece of paper which had been written on with phosphorescent paint. They could read it plainly in the dark.

"Outdated? Maybe.

"But I'm just a baby," was written on it.

"What does it mean?" Tracy asked.

"Search me! Leave it to Mr. Andrews! He's going to make this tough! Come on!" Once again he casually took Tracy's hand and they headed off toward the pool. They were groping their way in pitch blackness. The pool, with its underwater light, was a pale green oval below them. Tracy stumbled into a chaise and became separated from Jeep. Suddenly someone banged into her from the rear and she would have gone clear over had she not grabbed the chaise for support. A dark figure was etched against the pale light of the pool for an instant and was gone. They play rough around here, Tracy thought in outrage as she rubbed her skinned ankle. Then she wondered briefly why the person who'd knocked her over had been alone, but she dismissed the thought as she heard Jeep calling her.

It must have been fifteen minutes after she had

joined forces with Jeep and they had prowled the pool area together that Jeep found another clue.

"That's funny," he said. "Leaving it right on top of this table in almost plain sight. I wonder how the rest of 'em missed it." He picked it up and together they moved over by the diving board where there was enough light to read by.

"This is no game, rich man," the message read. "Your daughter is gone and you will hear later how much you'll have to pay to get her back. She's far away where you'll never find her. After this better not play any more fancy games in the dark, rich man." They looked up, searching each other's faces.

"I don't understand," Tracy said. "What kind of a hint or clue is that? It doesn't match up with the other one—"

Jeep's face was serious in the undulating light from the pool. "I don't think it's part of the game," he said. "I don't know—come on! Let's go up and tell Mr. Andrews!" He took off up the curving path toward the distant, sputtering Tiki torches.

"Tell him what?" Tracy muttered, stumbling after him. Crazy people—wandering around in the dark, leaving undecipherable messages. If this was how the other half lived, she preferred her own half!

"Mr. Andrews?" Jeep puffed when they finally got up to the terrace.

"That you, Jeep? I didn't expect even you this fast!"

57

"No. It's something else. Well—read this. Is this one of your clues?"

Mr. Andrews read the note quickly, and the color drained from his face. "No, it isn't," he said shortly. "We'd better call the others back right now." He went over to the table to get the whistle. "I just hope this is a not-very-funny joke!" He blew the whistle and in a short while returning footsteps pounded up the path and around the sides of the house. Mr. Andrews switched on the overhead lighting on the terrace.

"What's up?" Mary Hendricks asked, puffing and laughing. "Did somebody win already? We haven't even found one clue!" Mr. Andrews was busy looking over every figure as the young people came running to the terrace. Finally Craig Harrison dragged up the path. He collapsed in a chair.

"If anybody won it," he gasped. "I bet it was your own daughter! I haven't seen her since the game started!" Tracy drew in her breath.

"Are you sure?" Mr. Andrews said tightly.

"Yes," Craig said, straightening up in the chair. Everybody became very quiet.

"Has anyone seen her?" Mr. Andrews snapped. Nobody had.

"I don't know whether this means anything or not," Tracy said in a small voice. They all turned toward her. "But somebody knocked me down, and I noticed he was big and alone—" her voice trailed off as she stared up at Bart Andrews' sickened face.

"The game's called off," he said. "Sue's gone. I'm calling the sheriff." He wheeled and ran into the house. The young people exchanged frightened glances. But nobody mentioned the word, "kidnapped." Uncertainly they shuffled toward the house and walked into the den. Through the closed door into the hall they could hear Mr. Andrews' voice talking on the telephone over the muffled sobs of Mrs. Andrews. The nightmare quality of the whole situation affected all of them. They just sat around, no one knowing what to say or do.

Mr. Andrews came back in. "We've assembled all the servants to question them and the gardener's new helper is missing. Anybody seen him? A big, swarthy man?" They all shook their heads. Tracy's eyes were huge. The man she'd seen was enormous. "How could I have known?" Mr. Andrews said half to himself. "His references were all right. If he has hurt her—" He left the room abruptly.

In what seemed like five minutes they heard the scream of a siren, first faint and far away, then getting louder and louder. The front door opened and the group heard Mr. Andrews talking to two men. Then they came into the den and Tracy felt better the minute she saw the tall, competent-looking sheriff's deputies with Mr. Andrews. They all repeated where they had been and what they had seen, but apparently Tracy was the only one who had seen the man. When the questioning was over one of the deputies went back to the phone.

"I'm going to check in on the roadblocks," he told Mr. Andrews. "Calling in as fast as you did—I'm sure we'll get him before he can get very far." He left the room.

"I don't want any of you to leave here," the other deputy said. "We have enough to worry about without all you kids heading back to the city. Safest and best place for you is right here. You can go home when—" he hesitated slightly—"when we find Miss Andrews."

Judy and Mary and the rest of the girls excused themselves and went upstairs. The boys just sat around, trying to read. Two of them tried to start a card game, but gave it up because neither of them could concentrate on what he was doing. "If only we could do something!" one of them said into the uneasy silence. "The worst part is feeling so darned helpless!"

Tracy, who had not gone upstairs with the other girls, got up and went out through the open sliding door. She felt restless and upset and somehow the sight of all these worried boys upset her all the more. Mysterious houseparty, they had said. Nobody had realized just how mysterious it was going to be! She walked over beyond the irregular rim of light to a low white rail fence. She leaned on it and looked out across the pasture, now beginning to show up more clearly under the light of an apricot moon. It should have been a beautiful sight, but now the farm buildings looked eerie and vaguely threatening. Terror seemed to be everywhere.

"Pretty awful, isn't it?" a voice said right at her elbow and Tracy nearly jumped out of her skin. She recognized Jeep Hendricks' tall form, angled into a fence-resting position next to her.

"It certainly is!" she answered. "I'll bet Mr. Andrews is sorry now he ever had this big show-off mystery houseparty!" There was a short, loaded silence.

"I might have expected that from you," Jeep finally said, and his voice was low.

"What do you mean?" Tracy was astounded at the emotion in his voice.

"Show-off party!" he repeated venomously. "You don't realize that Bart Andrews is the most generous guy alive, do you? He gives this 'show-off' party, as you call it, and a lot of other things for all of us, and has been doing it all our lives. A guy with all his money and he still takes time for a bunch of kids his daughter is growing up with!" He moved over closer to Tracy. "I don't usually talk to girls like I'm going to talk to you," he went on, "but I think you're just about the worst snob I ever met in my whole life!"

"Snob!" Tracy gasped. "Me?"

"You bet, you! You haven't had a pleasant word for anybody since you got here, or even had a pleasant expression! What's the matter with being rich? Does that mean you're automatically a dirty guy? Some of these kids have money, some of them don't—but it doesn't make any difference. They're all great kids just the same. And that crack about being 'outside San Francisco'—Judy told us where you're from! Just how far out were you—country girl—300 miles?"

"Two hundred and fifty," Tracy said in a small voice. She was in a state of shock. First to be so terrified about what had happened to Sue—then to be bawled out by this big bully. She felt a tear slip down her cheek. Jeep didn't notice.

"Everybody's crazy about Judy," he went on, staring across the pasture. "And we could hardly wait to meet her cousin. I was really impressed when Judy introduced us back in the city." He paused. "Then you turn out to be a frozen-faced little snip with about as bad a case of reverse-snobbishness as I've ever seen!"

"That's not fair!" Tracy was finally stung into answering. "I am from the country! And I love it there and I loathe the city! You kids are such a—a closed corporation, and you always do everything right, and I—I belong in the sticks, not trying to be somebody like your sister—smooth and confident and perfect—"

"Well, now we're getting someplace," he said in a more reasonable voice. "Afraid you wouldn't fit in, so you wouldn't try at all, is that it?"

Tracy peered at him in the pale light. That was it! She realized as his words sunk in that she had wanted so to be like Judy and Mary in their environment that she had ended up not being anybody—least of all herself. Instead of being unwilling to share Crowley's Corners with them, Tracy now realized she had really been ashamed of it.

She turned away and stared off across the pasture as Jeep was doing. Her mind was in a turmoil. Everything Jeep had said to her she had had coming. She had been so smug—calling everybody else a phony when she had been the biggest phony of all. And Jeep knew it.

"This is terrible," she said in a low voice. "Here we are fighting about me, when I don't count at all. Not now, when Sue might be—" her voice failed her.

Surprisingly Jeep reached over and took her hand. "I'm sorry I was so hard on you," he said. "The truth is I'm scared to death about Sue and that remark of yours about show-off parties—well, it just set me off, I guess."

In spite of everything Tracy felt a warmth spreading through her generated by the warmth of Jeep's hand holding hers. "I had it coming," she said, then stopped. Something was wrong. As the moon climbed higher Tracy became surer that something was definitely wrong—some piece of the moon-washed jigsaw puzzle before them didn't fit, but she didn't know which one it was.

"What's the matter?" Jeep asked, looking down at her.

"I don't know. I have a funny feeling—" Together they stared out into the fields. "It seemed all right a few minutes ago," Tracy murmured. "But now—" There was a tense silence. Then, "*Jeep!*" she exclaimed, and it was his turn to jump.

"Gosh, what is it?"

"I know what it is! I know what's wrong! The arms of the windmill have stopped going around!"

"So they have," he said after a minute. "But so what? The wind isn't blowing anyway."

"Then why were they going around to beat the band a minute ago? Besides, nobody would use a regular windmill on a big place like this! Machinery does the pumping! But why did the windmill stop?" They stared at each other, then Tracy looked around nervously. "I wonder how far away that sheriff is? Somebody ought to get out there right now!"

Jeep already had one leg over the railing. Tracy started to climb over after him. "Oh, no, you don't!" he said. "This is man's work!"

"Listen! It was my idea, and I'm coming! You don't know straight up about windmills!"

"All right," he conceded. "But be quiet!"

Stealthily they crept across the open pasture. What were they going to find? Probably nothing, Tracy tried to tell herself, but her nerves were reacting differently. Every inch of her skin seemed alert and tense and seemed to crawl along her bones. If nothing were there, then why had the windmill stopped? Finally Jeep, a little way ahead of her, signaled for her to join him.

"I'm going around to the other side where the door is," he whispered. "I absolutely forbid you to come with me." Tracy nodded. She knew he meant it. She watched him slip through the grass, out of sight around the corner of the strangely, ominously silent windmill. Then quickly, as she had always done at home when sneaking up on a stubborn cow in the wrong field, she slipped over to the windmill. She stretched up on tip-toes and what she saw through the tiny, glassless window made her draw in her breath in shock. In the faint light filtering in through the open doorway she could see Sue, a rag over her mouth, her head slumped over her chest. She was tied to some piping coming from the machinery on the floor. A man who looked at least nine feet tall was standing over her, glaring down hideously.

"That might be a little more comfy than upstairs," Tracy could hear him growl. "Now I'm gonna turn on the motor so if you keep on fighting you're liable to end up as part of the machinery in this Dutch toy! Besides, we wouldn't want your dad to suspect nothing, now, would we?" Tracy watched him go over to a switch on the opposite wall and then she heard the groan and wheeze of the over-sized blades starting to grind around above them. A motor right near Sue's head began to throb. At that very moment both Tracy and the man saw Jeep's figure outlined in the doorway—a perfect target. The man emitted a guttural sound and started for him. Against a giant of a man like this he would have no chance. Tracy's fingers gripped the edge of the window and at that precise instant the air was pierced with an ear-splitting, terrifying sound loud and shattering enough to wake the dead. The man whirled in confusion as the last echo died away. Then he turned again toward Jeep who, instead of running, was standing out from the doorway a little farther. He looked up once, then grimaced at the man.

"Come out and get me!" he taunted. "If you're man enough!"

The man ran at him with an enraged howl and just as he got outside the door one of the huge wooden arms of the windmill swung around, and because of his tremendous size, caught him directly on top of his head. He fell like a tree.

Tracy ran around to the door and she and Jeep ducked under the revolving blades easily. They worked on the ropes that held Sue. Tracy put her head to her chest and she was breathing. Shallow breathing, perhaps, but she was alive. They finally got her arms free and there were ugly red welts where she had struggled against the ropes. Her eyelids fluttered and then terror shone out of her opened eyes.

"It's all right, Sue," Jeep told her softly. "You're going to be all right. The man is gone."

Slowly the panic seemed to leave her. "It—it was the gardener's helper," she said in a shaky voice. "He—he seemed to resent all of us. He kept talking about the horse as if that was the last straw. He said he'd keep me here, even if my dad did pay him the money—He was c-crazy—" her breath caught in a sob.

"Don't cry, Sue," Tracy said. "Don't even think about it." The poor kid was obviously delirious —muttering about a horse. Then there was a foreign sound above the motor and the grinding of the blades. Tracy looked up and there across the room was a beautiful Palomino horse tied up behind Sue in the shadows.

"What on earth—" she began.

Sue smiled tiredly. "That's Baby. He was to have been the prize in the game tonight. That's what set that madman off—"

"Never mind about it now, Sue," Tracy said firmly. She was so relieved that everything was all right she didn't even want to think about the game. "Can you walk? Let's get right back to your folks. They're scared half out of their wits."

Helped by Jeep on one side and Tracy on the

other they struggled across the meadow. Finally Jeep lifted Sue over the railing and Tracy ran ahead to tell the others. Mrs. Andrews was seated in the den, her head bowed. Mr. Andrews was talking to the sheriff on the telephone in the hall.

"It's all right!" Tracy gasped, running into the den. "We found her! Jeep is bringing her in now. She's all right! The gardener had her tied up in the windmill—"

Jeep walked in carrying Sue. Her mother rushed over to her and the joy on her face was something Tracy knew she would never forget. She ran to the hall and told Sue's father. He managed to blurt the news to the sheriff, then rushed into the den. The other girls, roused by all the excitement, came trailing down the stairs. Sue smiled wanly at everybody from the sofa.

"The sheriff's coming right over to get him," Mr. Andrews announced after he had made sure that Sue was all right.

"No need to hurry," Jeep said, "I don't think he'll be going any place for awhile."

"What I can't understand," Mr. Andrews said then, "is why didn't the deputies find you when they searched the windmill?"

Sue's face clouded. "When he heard somebody coming," she said with an effort, "he dragged me up to a little platform just opposite the center of the windmill blades. He was so big he could climb up

68

there, and from the ground it—it looked like a ceiling."

"That's what he meant when he said something about upstairs," Tracy said. Jeep got up from Sue's side and crossed to Tracy.

"And the reason we went out to the windmill," he said, "is because Tracy here noticed the arms had stopped revolving, and she figured something must be wrong. It was all her idea." Everyone looked at her, and the stares that Tracy had always interpreted as who-are-you now looked like we-like-you.

"Well, Tracy," Mr. Andrews said, "you win the prize! And you won it fair and square. You found Baby and Sue by a clue even the sheriff and I missed!"

Tracy stared at him. That beautiful Palomino to be hers? Her very own horse? "Gosh!" was all that she could say.

"But, wait!" Jeep said suddenly. "What on earth was that ungodly noise? That horrible screech that made the guy turn so I could get him out where the windmill would clobber him?"

Tracy cleared her throat. "Well," she began, "it was the only thing I could think of to do. I'm afraid that was the champion hog caller of Crowley's Corners!"

Tracy joined them all in a hearty laugh. When the last giggle had died away Jeep put his arm around her shoulder.

"Well, I don't know about the rest of you," he said, "but speaking for the Andrews family and myself—I'm awfully glad my date this weekend is a country girl!"

And One for the Road

THE air sizzled with excitement. The Junior Racers, cheeks red and eyes glistening, were getting ready for the big one, the Giant Slalom. They had been training hard, and every boy and girl was bent on victory. Their equipment was in top condition and the skis were filed and waxed until they glistened.

They were chattering and talking a little too brightly, keyed up like race horses waiting at the gate. The sky looked threatening, but that did not dull their spirits. Some new powder snow on top of a firm base is the skier's dream.

Stu and Sally were sitting at a small corner table, talking quietly, sipping their hot chocolate. Stu went over to the vending machine and got a couple of Almond Joys.

"One's to eat, and one for the road," he said, smiling, as he eased his big frame back into the chair.

Sally wrinkled her cute nose. "You and your candy bars! If you had just one dime left to spend, I'll wager you'd blow it all on candy!"

"You're just jealous. You're chicken to spoil your pretty figure."

Laughingly they pushed back their chairs. Nancy put on her gold quilt parka and pulled the hood over her dark wavy hair. Stu let out an involuntary whistle as he pulled his own blue jacket over his broad shoulders.

"You know, a fellow could get smug, knowing you were his girl."

"That's what I like about you, Stu, always thinking of the gallant thing to say!"

She started to walk around the table and then stopped. A large, heavy-set fellow with a blue stocking mask over his face brushed past.

"Hm, you'd think those masks would get awfully warm indoors—but they must be nice and snug out there, especially when it's snowing," Sally said as they walked out.

The rest of the skiers were getting ready, putting on their skis and starting off for the chair lift. "See you on top!" they called out as they left.

Stu tried to fasten his bindings, but something was wrong—they wouldn't close. He jiggled and pushed down with all his strength.

"Oh, neat! That's a bad break. You better run along, Sally—no sense both of us being late."

Sally hesitated, but most of the skiers had left. "All right, Stu, but you hurry up and I'll see you on top!"

"Yeah, see you at the top," he mumbled glumly as the lift carried the last of them out of sight. The snow was falling lightly now, but through the thin white veil he could still see Sally's red leather glove raised in a gay wave. And then they were gone.

He worked feverishly with his screwdriver and file. The races always started on time, and no quarter given. Suddenly, with a small ping, the offending piece of ice worked loose, hitting him on the side of his upturned nose.

"Whew, at last!" and he wiped his parka sleeve across his forehead, his blue eyes full of anxiety. With any luck at all he might still make it! As he stooped to put on his skis he noticed Sally's red scarf in the snow, stuffed it in his pocket, and he was off.

Luckily there wasn't much of a line, and in just a minute he had settled into the double chair, poles under his arm, and legs and skis dangling. He fastened the safety strap and leaned back comfortably, still warm from the rush and exertion. The snow was coming down somewhat harder now and the world was quiet and peaceful.

Stu looked at the fellow beside him. "Say, that's pretty neat, wearing one of those face masks on the chair—that ought to keep your face from chapping."

But his neighbor just stared straight ahead. Stu thought he hadn't heard and looked more closely.

"Say, how do you like using snow-shoes? Must be quite a change from skis."

Still no answer.

Well, so much for the companionship of the hill, Stu thought, and settled back for a long quiet trip. Actually, this was the longest lift in the High Sierras, 3,000 ft. rise on a two-and-a-half mile run, and it made possible the most thrilling down-hill runs Stu had ever known. It was well worth the long cold ride up.

The others must be up there now. He wished the chair would go faster. It seemed to be creeping. The little stubby pine tops way below seemed to be standing still, almost. And then he noticed! The feel of motion had slowed down, and the little whirring noise the wheel made at the top of the chair as it traveled over the cable eased down, and then stopped.

"Oh, no, not that!" he groaned, completely tense and frustrated now. Nothing to do but wait for it to start again.

"Eh, got some grub, Joe?"

Stu looked up startled. The blue stocking mask was turned towards him, bland and without expression, with two little white circles outlining the eyes, and two little white circles for nose tip and mouth. Over this was a gray hood, attached to a heavy jacket such as loggers wear. Heavy gray khaki pants were bunched and pushed into a pair of high black loggers' boots from which hung the snow-shoes.

"I ask ya, bub, ya got some grub?"

Stu fumbled with the zipper of his large pocket. "I have an apple here," he said, reluctant to part with his "emergency ration." At least he still had the candy bar.

"O.K. give it!" the hooded voice came through.

"Well, that's that," Stu thought sadly, and then he froze in sudden alarm as the fellow yanked a switch blade from his boot. It cut the air with a silvery flash as the man sprung it open. Calmly he pointed it and then sunk it straight into the heart of the apple, cleaving it exactly in two. He deftly speared one half atop the steel blade and pointed it at Stu.

"Here, kid."

Stu reached out mechanically with his mittened hand and awkwardly took the piece. The man wiped the blade clean on his khaki pants and, in the same motion, had it back in his boot.

Fascinated, Stu stared as the man lifted his mask just enough to clear his mouth, but in that moment Stu saw the bright red scar that ran along the left side of the man's mouth, and down to his chin.

He busied himself with the apple, hoping the man had not seen him stare, or his look of sudden recognition. But the man had already gulped the apple and lowered the mask.

"Slow now, boy, easy does it!" Stu thought, thankful that the chair was bobbing again and the little wheel humming. So long as the man did not know he had been recognized, Stu felt he would be reasonably safe. He made himself eat the apple, slowly, trying to keep busy as long as possible. He had to think of what to do once they arrived at the top.

Stu had no doubt that his menacing partner was Don Molay, escaped convict. The successful jail-break had been in all the papers and Molay's picture on the front page with special attention to the bright red scar which was the result of his fight with a prison guard. He was described as armed and very dangerous.

With the whole country looking, he, Stu, was the only one who knew the whereabouts of Don Molay! And much too close for comfort.

Finally the chair arrived at the top and the man and the boy eased themselves onto the snow. The man immediately started up the hill on his snow-shoes. Stu bent down and busied himself with his bindings. He could see the racers down below, but no one near to signal or leave a message. He didn't dare wait. The snow would soon fill in the wide flat snow-shoe tracks, and already the outline of the man was growing dim. One more moment, and

Stu was on his way, keeping a steady distance between himself and the convict. If he could keep from losing the man, he could find the hideout and return safely to get help. It should be simple. The skis moved ahead without a sound and the screen of falling snow would keep him well hidden.

Up and up they went, the man doggedly pacing into the storm, heavy footed, leaving an oval webbed mark at every step, and the boy tense in every muscle, intent on just one goal. The man was slowing down now and then Stu saw the tiny cabin, almost hidden in the snow. A small blue plume of smoke was coming from the chimney, bent over under the falling snow. So this was the hide-away, probably put up years ago by some enterprising hikers.

Stu had learned all he needed to know and started to turn around.

"Okay, bub, that's as far as ya go!"

Stu looked up. The man had reached the cabin door and was standing there, legs wide-spread, a rifle in his hand.

"You wouldn't dare shoot!" Stu looked straight at him. "A shot up here would be heard clear through the valley, and you might even start an avalanche!"

"Mebbe you're right, Joe. But I also got me a knife that can go easy to where you're at, and it never misses. Best ya just come up here. And when ya get to three yards from this here door take off them skis and leave 'em. I'll take good care of 'em for ye."

Stu came on slowly—he hadn't figured on this. He took off his skis and went through the narrow door. Inside it was nearly dark. He could make out a pot-bellied stove and a bunk over to one side. There were no windows and the only light came from the doorway.

The man pointed to a three-legged stool, "Okay, Joe, sit right there. Nothin' will happen to ya so long's ya behave. Ya ain't goin' far in this snow without skis, and I got them taken care of. Ain't about to have a young snoop tell where I'm at."

Stu sat down. The man was right. Without snow-shoes or skis he would sink into the new snow up to his hips and there wasn't a chance of making it down the mountain. He'd have to hope and wait for a chance.

Molay had set himself to work fixing some food on top of the old black stove. He put a can of pork and beans on there and a pan of snow from the stoop to heat for coffee. Stu was surprised that it smelled so good. If only he still had his "emergency rations!"

Molay handed him a tin plate and cup. "Okay, bub, have some grub." Then he wolfed down his own food, keeping a furtive eye on Stu all the time.

Next he threw a bunch of blankets on the floor, right in front of the door.

"I'll sleep right here, Joe, you take the bunk, and

don't try nothin'. Sure thought I'd be safe up here another week or two."

The bunk was hard and uncomfortable as Stu turned and twisted. He couldn't tell if Molay was asleep or awake. There wasn't a sound, but he had an eerie feeling he was being watched. Stu shuddered under the heavy wool blanket. He had to keep awake! He fingered the screwdriver and the file, the only weapons he had. They would be little protection against a twelve-inch switch blade which Molay seemed to know just how to handle.

Stu had no idea how long he had lain there. Suddenly he stiffened. He had sensed, rather than heard, some movement across the room. He strained his eyes in the dark and then he saw the bulky shadow between him and the stove, coming closer, slowly, heavily, but without a sound.

"This is it!" he thought, closing his eyes and trying to shrink deeper into the scratchy blanket. His clenched hand felt clammy around the pointed file —he could hear the man's breathing now and could feel his nearness. Suddenly he felt the beam of a flashlight fully on his face. Stu did not stir and kept his eyes closed tight, trying to keep his breathing regular. It seemed like ages and then the light was off and the man moving away.

Stu stifled a gasp of relief! Don Molay had only been checking. Stu wondered what had kept him from panicking and giving himself away?

Twice more during that long night, when Stu

had finally drifted into a restless sleep, he was disturbed by that beam of light, but though he was still frightened, it was easier now to lie still and make believe he was asleep.

There was no way of telling when morning had arrived, except that Molay was moving about in his heavy but noiseless way. He opened the door and scooped up snow, and Stu got a glimpse of dim daylight. Molay was making coffee and flapjacks when he motioned Stu to sit down on the wooden stool and, without a word, handed him the tin plate and cup. The cakes were delicious.

"You sure know how to make pancakes," Stu said. The man was wolfing his food noisily and then licked his lips. He wiped his shirt sleeve across his mouth, and even in the dimness Stu could make out the bright red scar.

"Yeah, Gramps taught me when I was little. Maw and Paw were dead. But Gramps was tops. Used to take me huntin' and fishin' and things." He leaned back on the bunk and Stu thought he had finished. But then the raspy voice continued.

"One day him and me was separated and I thought I heard a deer arustlin'. I took aim and shot." A longer pause this time, and then, quietly:

" 'T were my own Gramps I had shot, and I laid down and I bawled and bawled, with him lying there with blood running down his side. And then I picked m'self up and ran and ran.

"Guess I must've run all day till I got to a big

80

city, and I was scared and hid. Slept in a basement or an empty building. Sometimes I'd find food and other times I'd just take some. And once in a while I'd find an odd job.

"There were others just like me and we went together. We'd find jobs, and if there wasn't any, we'd find food or take things. And then we figured it was easier takin' things. Nobody could find us 'cause we knew all the places to hide. So we kept on takin', or we'd get in a store at night. We had plenty of spendin' money then and were real smart —and then one day we figured a bank would be the easiest yet."

Stu was sure the older man had forgotten he was there. He listened in fascination.

"Mebbe if we'd had a little learnin' we could have done it better—but it sure went sour. The alarm went off, and the sirens screamed and they hauled us away. And did they pin it on us! Most o' the ones we'd done, and plenty others besides.

"Jail is no place for one that's never had a boss. I couldn't stand it. I fought and fought, and each time they'd add on more time. I just couldn't stand it no more! I had to get out an' get back to the mountains like Gramps and me used to."

Stu listened, spellbound. He looked at the man leaning back on the bunk. This wasn't a murderer, just a guy who'd never had a chance. But now that Don Molay had finally gotten his life's wish, he surely wouldn't let Stu spoil it!

As if answering Stu's thought the man said, "And now that I got it made, you have to come along! I can't let anybody spoil this for me! You know, Joe, I can't let you go back, so ya'll have to stay here with me. After a while I'll find me another place, and then I'll let you go."

He went over to the stove and poured himself another cup of coffee. "Nobody here tells me what to do, and I like it that way, see?"

The man and the boy sat quietly across from each other, no telling how long, because time meant nothing inside the dark cabin. Stu was growing restless. There had to be some way out of this. He had no idea what the man had done with his skis and, as he had said, there was no use trying to make it through the new powder. The man's snow-shoes were hung on the wall near the door, but every move Stu made, the man was watching, alert as a cat ready to spring. Stu would just have to wait. By this time his friends and his family must be frantic, but how on earth would they know where to look for him in this tremendous snow wilderness?

Molay moved over to the door and opened it. He stood in the doorway looking at the heavy gray sky.

"Can't see the sun but it must be gettin' near noon." He bent over, scooping up some more snow, and suddenly Stu jumped up, ran at the man from behind knocking him over, and tried to reach for the snow-shoes. Molay reached out from below and caught Stu's ankle and held it like a vise. Stu kicked at the hand with his free foot in the heavy ski boot. The man howled with pain—and Stu, off balance, staggered and was almost out of the door. No time for the snow-shoes now! He slammed the door hard and jumped clear, just in time to avoid a mountain of snow dislodged by the jarring door, and which settled like a cascade on top of Don Molay.

Stu threw himself on the snow and tried to roll down. Molay would shake himself out in a moment, and he had to get away from that switch blade!

The snow was deep and soft, and rolling got his nose and eyes filled up, blinding and choking him without getting any real speed. One thing skiing had taught him was how to fall and change direction. He pulled up his knees to form a ball and flipped his weight and was now scooting away in a sitting position. He could now look around—and here came Molay, snow-shoes in hand, and even at that distance his face showed bright red.

Stu rolled again. It put less weight on the snow and was faster, and fright and desperation made him ignore the horrible freezing, scratching snow that seemed to burn out his eyes and nose. He couldn't do it more than a few seconds. When he flipped up again, Molay was catching up—still too far for the switch blade, but closing the gap fast. This wouldn't do!

Stu looked frantically around for anything that

might help him get away. He saw some cut up logs over on the right by the trees. Could he get to them? And would they help? He looked around again—Molay was closing in! Whatever he did better be fast!

He went down again, trying to roll at an angle to the right. When he came to a stop he was still a good ten yards from the logs and nothing to do but try to run it. He straightened up, but his legs sank down past his knees, and bruised as he was by now, it was torture to pick up each leg in turn, thrust it forward and sink in again. And oh, it was slow! He looked around—he had only seconds left and he could see the look of triumph on Molay's face.

Frantically he pushed on. His chest hurt at every breath and his body felt numb. This must be a nightmare! And there were the logs—just one more big step now—"Come on, Stu, you can make it!" He dragged himself over. He pushed and tugged with the strength of desperation, and the top log wiggled.

"O.K., kid, I gotcha now!" He heard the yell as he gave one more desperate push and the log rolled off and started down. Stu threw himself on it, feeling the hard impact as he hit, and held on for dear life. Faster, faster now the thing went sliding. He could hear the rasping yells behind him but he didn't dare look around. He dragged his legs in an effort to hold his "bobsled" and finally managed to steer it to a slightly less hazardous angle.

"Good heavens, won't this thing ever stop?!" At every bump his insides quaked. But he was free, free!

Why couldn't he just throw himself clear? The Lodge couldn't be too far below and he couldn't hold on any longer. Tensing every muscle, he kicked off and landed spread eagled on his back while the log continued on its horrendous course.

He lay there a moment, dazed, and then tried to get up. But something was wrong. His left leg buckled under and a searing hot pain shot through him. Good Lord, now what? He had put a good distance between him and Don Molay, but not enough to just lie there. Certainly he had left a wide enough trail for Molay to follow!

With superhuman effort he managed to sit up. He looked around him and then he spotted a weasel coming straight up the grade. He waved frantically, still afraid to shout. This must be the ski patrol—and they had spotted him. Slowly but steadily the weasel worked its way towards him. He could see now that there were several people on it, and it looked as if they were carrying guns.

And he saw Sally waving, "Stu, Stu, are you all right?"

"Guess we'd better get him down to the Lodge first," he heard someone say as they eased him on to a stretcher, and the pain was almost too much.

"No," he pointed. "Up the hill."

"I can put a splint on you while we're going. But are you sure you can make it?"

Stu gritted his teeth and held tight to Sally's hand as they rumbled up the mountain side.

"You know, that's the best lookin' gold parka I ever saw." His lopsided grin looked a little thin.

It wasn't hard to locate the snow-shoe tracks and follow them when Stu had pointed the way. And then they saw him. A lonely little black spot in all that white vastness, trying to get down the other side of the mountain as fast as he could.

When they came close enough to call, he stopped, tired and exhausted.

"All right. Come take me back. But I'm glad I come here anyhow. It was worth it!" and then, softly, "Guess they'll keep me the rest o' my life now." And the heavy man pulled himself aboard.

"But, Sally," the Sheriff asked as they rode back, "how could you be so sure Don Molay was up here?"

"That was easy. When I got to the top after the first race yesterday, I found where Stu had left my red scarf. What puzzled me was that Stu had left his Almond Joy on it, all cut up in pieces with the wrapper still around them. Stu wouldn't leave his candy bar! So I looked again—and there it was all spelled out with the cut up candy: 'D-O-N M-O-L-A-Y'.

"I was first to go, in the second race, and in my rush to get help, I set a new record. But by the time we located the Sheriff and got a search party together, it was getting dark. So we had to wait. I was terribly worried about you, Stu."

"I know half a dozen hikers' cabins hereabouts," the Sheriff said, "so we tried the closest ones first, but no luck. Then we found you. Sure hope your leg won't be too bad. You know, there's a real nice reward out for Molay here."

Stu turned to Sally. "So you set a brand-new record, eh?"

"So did you, my friend, so did you!" And she bent over to give him a big hug and a kiss.

Stu blushed to the roots of his sandy hair. "Whee, who needs a reward, anyhow?"

Sally fumbled with her zipper pocket. "Oh, by the way, I brought you a candy bar. I thought you might need it."

Day After Donna

————◆————◆————◆————

A. M. LIGHTNER

HIS name was Mr. Horace J. Means, but he was Old Man Meany to us. Because of his disposition and his attitude towards us, we'd called him that for as long as I can remember.

Old Man Meany's house is about three down from the Waterview Stand where all us hot-rodders hang out. It's one of those Revolutionary antiques, and it sure looked it—even before the flood. The Library Ladies were always trying to get it away from him so they could fix it up and turn it into a National Shrine, but he said that was where he was born and that was where he was going to die. And although he was so fat that what Dad calls his life expectancy must have been almost zero, still the Library Ladies were scared he'd live just long enough so the house would fall down on top of him and there wouldn't be anything left for a Shrine.

I guess he was plenty mean to the Library Ladies, but at the time it seemed to me he kept all his meanness for us. There'd no sooner be two or three of us down at the Waterview, showing off the latest thing we'd done to the motor or the nifty headlights we'd picked up or how she could stop on a dime, when down comes Old Man Meany to complain that we're making too much noise. Or if we all go in the Stand for a coke and nobody's making a peep, then he complains about how the joint looks with all those wrecks in front.

"Keep 'em away from my place!" he'd fume, when nobody thought of going near his old house.

He complained so much to the Town Council that they put a policeman on at the bridge. They said it was a dangerous corner, though there were hardly any cars around but ours. There was nothing for the policeman to watch but us, and that sure put a damper on everything. Couple of guys got pulled in for just rodding around a little, and they lost their licenses for half a year. After that Old Man Meany didn't think it wise to come in and complain. He just walked down to the bridge now and then and jawed with the policeman.

The flood was one of those things that happen once in fifty or a hundred years, which was why nobody expected it or believed it when it did happen. My dad said that if folks had watched the weather charts and kept an eye on a hurricane called Donna that blew up the coast—but the day was so bright and sunny and somehow you can't believe in disaster on a day like that.

Mom saw me go by the kitchen door and she looked out and called, "As long as you've got to risk your neck in that thing, please bring me back a loaf of pumpernickel."

I said right-ho and went on and started up the old bus, and if Mom said anything else, I didn't hear it.

I got down to the Waterview Stand and quite a number of the gang were already there. Chet had his roadster that his parents bought him when he graduated from High. And Stutz Loganberry had his stock car that he's been going to drive in the last six races at the County, only there's been something wrong every time. Last time the radiator leaked. But what really interested me was that Hank Miller was there with his '32 Ford. I hadn't seen Hank for almost a week, and I was anxious to see what he'd done to his motor. So he opened up the hood and we all poked our noses down his four-barrelled carbs, and there was plenty of talk about how he'd hopped her up and how much she could be expected to do, when all of a sudden I heard someone say:

"They aren't letting anyone across the bridge now."

We all straightened up at that. Nobody had been

paying the river much mind. Oh, we could hear her roaring there, and I'd noticed a little water was coming over the road at the low spot. But that happens every spring and fall regular.

"What do you mean?" I demanded, and started toward the bridge. I had just remembered the pumpernickel, and all the stores are on the other side of the river. Our side is strictly residential.

"There's a flood going on," someone said, as though I couldn't see it with my own eyes.

The water was higher up on the bridge than I'd ever seen it before, and it was dark and murky and full of floating pieces of wood—even parts of houses. Still, it didn't look to me like the bridge was in any danger.

"Look, Mr. Johnson," I said to our cop, who had suddenly become the guard for the bridge, "I won't be five minutes. I promised Mom I'd get her some pumpernickel. I'll just run over and run right back."

"Sorry, Tom," said Mr. Johnson. "The bridge is closed. Your Mom will have to wait till after the flood."

"But that's crazy," I protested. "Nothing's going to happen in five minutes."

Mr. Johnson looked like he was getting tired of saying the same thing but knew he was going to have to go on saying it a lot longer.

"Look, son," he said. "I could let you go over, though it's against my orders. But they wouldn't let

92

you come back. Sure as shooting, you'd have to stay there for the duration. Want that?"

"How long's this thing supposed to last?" I asked.

"Crest's expected at 2 o'clock," he replied, as though he'd said that a lot of times, too.

I gave up then. I could wait till 2 o'clock, I thought, when all the excitement would be over. I'd have lunch at the Stand and take Mom her pumpernickel in time for supper.

We stood and watched the river then. Quite a little crowd had gathered by the bridge, and we could see another crowd on the other side. I began to think old Johnson was right. Even if nothing happened to the bridge, you weren't going to be able to reach it from this side much longer. Not without getting your feet wet, you weren't.

The thought struck us all at the same time. We were trying to see who could pick out the most interesting item going down the river, when all at once we all yelled, "The rods!" and made a dash for them.

"Better get my roadster out of here!" Chet cried.

"A flood's no place for the winning number!" called Stutz, as he started his engine.

By this time we were all starting up and it sort of discouraged conversation. But Mrs. Mahoney, who runs the Waterview, came to the door. She's used to raising her voice to talk over the noise.

"Where you boys going?" she demanded. "You don't think the flood's coming this high, do you?"

"We're not taking any chances, Mrs. Mahoney," I shouted. "Not with this baby!"

"Not after I worked a week to change the rear-end," yelled Hank.

Mrs. Mahoney went back into the shop. I heard her shouting at her husband, and as I wheeled off after the gang, I saw Mr. Mahoney come out and get into his new Chevie. I knew he'd have no trouble parking it. But some folks object to what they call "junk" in front of their houses. Of course, now that Chet had his roadster it sort of lent class to the gang, though it wasn't the kind of class that appealed to me.

We had some argument about how far to go. Stutz thought along the canal would be all right. But when we hit the road to the canal we had to go through water, and Hank and Chet insisted on going farther. Once they went the rest of us followed, even though it meant farther to walk back. We all knew we were going back. Without saying anything, we realized this flood was going to be something to remember. We went quite a way beyond the canal and found a farmer who let us park in his field.

When we walked back over the canal bridge, we saw Mr. Mahoney. He was just taking the keys out of his car and he looked up at us in surprise.

"Where'd you boys move to?" he asked. "You don't think the river will come this high, do you?"

"Better safe than sorry," Chet said.

"Don't want anything to keep us from that race on Sunday," Stutz added.

"And after all the work I just put in . . ." continued Hank.

Mr. Mahoney laughed, but I thought it had a nervous edge.

"Let's be realistic," he said. "Whoever heard of the river coming this far? Well, now you've put them there, might as well leave 'em. Come along with me, boys. I hear the Fire Department needs men."

When we got to the firehouse, we found it set up as Flood Relief and Rescue Headquarters. The National Guard and the Red Cross hadn't arrived yet—they came later and sort of took over what the Fire Department had started. The Fire Chief, Mr. Nelson, was talking on the telephone and answering questions and giving directions all at once. He looked up as we followed Mr. Mahoney in, and said:

"We've got to get up the river fast, Bill. Those children's camps have to be evacuated."

Mr. Mahoney said, "I brought these boys along. I thought since they know all about car motors some of them might understand an outboard."

"That so?" asked Chief Nelson. "Any of you boys know how to run a boat? Any of you got a boat you can run?"

It turned out that Chet's parents had a boat and Stutz knew all about outboards. So they went off with Chief Nelson to get the boat and rescue the campers, and Hank and I were told to go with Mr. Mahoney and help people in our village.

"Got to get everyone out of the houses along the river," Mr. Mahoney said. "You boys take the ones upriver and I'll go down."

We set out walking. The road was under water by this time and our feet were plenty wet. First house we went to there was old Mrs. Miller digging in her garden. The water hadn't quite reached her but it was getting there. I'd never heard she was going blind, but now I began to wonder.

"Excuse me, Mrs. Miller," I said. "We've been told to get everyone out of these houses. We'll help you up to the firehouse and you'll be safe there till the flood's over."

"What's that, sonny?" she asked. "Yes, I know there's a flood. I'm just digging up these bulbs so the water won't get to them. I'll leave them in this basket on the kitchen table."

"We're told to hurry everyone along," Hank said.

We watched as she went on digging. What can you do if you're a teenager and an adult won't hurry?

"Chief Nelson said . . ." I began.

"You tell Chief Nelson I'll be right there," she replied without looking up, "just as soon as I finish this bed."

"There won't be any bed pretty soon . . ." Hank began, but I pulled him along.

"We've told her," I said. "Let's go to the next house."

At the next one Mr. Buxton was cutting his hedge.

"Today's the day for hedge-trimming," he said. "About due, don't you think? Oh, the flood? I'll get it done before I get my feet wet. Don't you boys worry."

Mr. Buxton looked as though he could swim out, which I doubted about old Mrs. Miller. We left him cutting his hedge and went on, and then we were staring at Old Man Meany's. Neither of us wanted to tackle him, but I told myself this was an emergency and went up to the door. Mr. Means met me with a pile of books in his arms.

"What you boys want? Of course I know there's a flood. Moved everything out of my cellar an hour ago. Now I'm moving up to the second floor. And I don't need any help from you!"

"Mr. Means," I said, "nobody knows how high she'll go."

"Oh, they don't? Well, she won't go too high for this old house. Stood worse floods than this, I can tell you. I'm surprised to see you boys separated from your jalopies."

"Oh, we put them in a safe spot, other side of the canal," Hank told him.

"What a pity!" said Old Man Meany. "I sort of hoped they'd gone down the river!" And he shut the door in our faces.

I don't mean to say that all the people were like that. Most of them came right along and some of them offered to help and practically all of them thanked us. When we got done routing them all out, we helped move the Post Office. That took a lot of time and the post mistress later got a citation for not letting a single letter get lost, even though the Post Office itself went down the river.

By the time we got done, the Red Cross had arrived and was serving soup in the firehouse. Hank and I had some and listened to reports of the campers being rescued upriver and we sort of envied Chet and Stutz. When we went out again the water was so high you couldn't walk in the road anymore. At least it was a lot easier to use a boat. And before I knew it, somebody was pushing Hank and me into a rowboat with an outboard and telling us to go look for anyone that needed rescuing. Just about then I remembered Mom and the pumpernickel.

"What happened to the crest?" I asked the man in charge. "I thought it was coming at 2 o'clock."

"We hope," he said. "2 A.M. o'clock. It's only 4 P.M. now."

Holy smokes! I could see that if it was going to go on rising till 2 A.M., and it was this high now, an awful lot more was going to be under water. I got the use of the phone for a minute and told Mom to forget the pumpernickel and not to worry about me. And then Hank and I pushed off with the outboard.

It certainly was strange to be going up and down the main drag in a boat. Most of the people had walked out before it was too late. But we rescued several cats and dogs and we helped move a lot of feed bags from the mill. When the water got too high there, we went back to the Waterview Stand and helped Mr. and Mrs. Mahoney. I felt real sorry for them. Everything they had was in that house and you couldn't possibly move it all out. We helped them take things up from the basement and then up to the second floor. When I looked at the food and the equipment and thought of all the hotdogs and sodas that we wouldn't have there anymore, I nearly bust out crying. I guess Mr. Mahoney felt the same way. One time as we were taking a breather, he looked at us and said,

"I got to hand it to you kids. You're smart, putting your cars in that field."

We'd just heard the news that the river had met the canal.

"If you'll give me your keys," I told him, "I'll try to move your car."

"I'd go myself if there was any use," he said.

By the time it got dark the water was so high we knew we couldn't stay any longer in the Waterview. We'd have to leave things as they were and just pray. Mrs. Mahoney had already gone to help with the Red Cross. Mr. Mahoney, Hank and I climbed out the second floor window into the boat. We looked at the old Stand in the light of the flashlight and we all were hoping it would be there in the morning. I was also wondering what had happened to Mr. Buxton's hedge and whether old Mrs. Miller's bulbs were still in the basket on her kitchen table. And just then we heard someone hollering from up the river.

"That's funny," said Mr. Mahoney. "I thought everyone was out of those houses. Didn't you boys get 'em all out?"

"We told everyone and helped the ones that needed it. But some of them wouldn't go right away. Some of them had things to do."

"Things, my eye!" grunted Mr. Mahoney.

"Like old Mrs. Miller," put in Hank. "She was digging her bulbs. And Mr. Buxton was cutting his hedge."

"I saw both of them at the relief kitchen. Who else wouldn't go?"

"Well, there was Old Man . . . I mean, Mr. Means. He didn't want to have anything to do with us."

"That's who it is all right," said Mr. Mahoney. "Let's get up there. About three houses, isn't it?"

We turned the boat around and Hank got the motor going and we headed for Old Man Meany's house. Sure enough, he was leaning out an upstairs window, yelling to beat the band. I don't know just what he was yelling. There was so much noise with

the river roaring and every once in awhile something heavy would hit the house and a shower of
bricks and slates would rattle down. We steered the
boat a little above the house and let the current
carry us down, and Mr. Mahoney reached out and
grabbed hold of something, a vine or the edge of
the window. It was too dark to see and I knew
we wouldn't stay there very long.

"Hurry up and climb in, Means!" Mr. Mahoney
told him. "Lucky we heard you. I thought we'd
cleared everyone out of these houses long ago."

But Mr. Means had disappeared inside the house
and Mr. Mahoney was talking to an empty window.
Mr. Mahoney swore.

"You all right, Means?" he yelled. "Hurry up! I
can't hold on here long."

The outboard sputtered and Hank was having
trouble keeping it going and holding us right at
that window, and I knew that if the motor died
we'd be half way through the town in no time and
in a heck of a mess.

"You know what I think's wrong, Mr. Mahoney?"
I said. "I bet he's too fat to get through the window. I bet he's worried about that."

"That's ridiculous!" cried Mr. Mahoney. "He can
squeeze through if he tries."

"You know these Revolutionary houses," Hank
said. "They sure skimped on the windows."

"Hurry up, Means!" Mahoney yelled again. "Do

you want the house to float off while we're waiting?"

There was a muffled exclamation from inside, something that sounded like "I can't! I can't!" Mr. Mahoney took a firmer hold on the window and peered in.

"I guess you'd better go in after him, Tom," he said. "Maybe you can push him out."

Now that was just what I did not want to do. At the rate the slates were sliding off the roof and the bricks off the chimney, I could see that one possible National Shrine was not going to be there in the morning. I didn't want to be a hero, but if I had to, why did it have to be rescuing Old Man Meany? However, there was Mr. Mahoney holding the boat steady and Hank pushing it closer to the window while he nursed the motor, and both of them saying, "Watch your step! In you go!" And before I knew it, I was in Old Man Meany's upstairs bedroom.

It was so dark in there that I couldn't see a thing at first. The electricity had been off for hours, of course, and the only light was a tiny candle. The room was packed with books and extra furniture that he had moved up from downstairs, and I could just make out Old Man Meany bending over the bed.

When he saw me he burbled something like, "Thank you, thank you!" and I thought he was go-

ing to start saying his prayers. Then I saw he was
tugging at the bed.

"Just help me with the mattress," he said. "Can't
go without the mattress!"

Well, I thought he really was off his rocker. But
if a guy goes crazy in an emergency and you have
to get him through a hole that's too small for him,
you humor him to begin with.

"Look, Mr. Means," I said. "There's lots of mat-
tresses down at the Red Cross. Much better mat-
tresses. You just leave that one here and we'll see
that you get a new one to sleep on."

"Not without the mattress!" Old Man Meany
started to yell, and I really thought he was going
into a frenzy. "This mattress! Gotta have this mattress! Didn't you come in here to help, young fellow?"

"That's what I'm trying to do," I said, "but you
won't let me. I've been telling you all day this house
isn't safe, but you wouldn't listen. Now you've
waited so long you'll have to go out the window.
But if you'll just let me push you, we'll get you
there yet."

"Not without the mattress!" he wailed. "Come on
and help me roll it up."

"But we haven't time for the mattress or room
for the mattress! And I keep telling you, the Red
Cross is being awfully good to everyone. They're
giving out dozens and dozens . . ."

"Young fellow," said Old Man Meany, "come

here!" And he grabbed me by the arm and pulled me over to the bed. "Feel in there," he said, "but don't grab." And he pushed my hand into a hole in the mattress.

I didn't need a light to realize there was more in that mattress than stuffing. I could tell the feel of good old dollar bills even in the dark. Then it came to me that if they were much bigger than one-dollar bills, there was an awful lot of green stuff in that mattress.

Old Man Meany was going on in a sort of desperate sing-song beside me.

"All my life's work! All my savings, scrimpings, sacrifices for my old age!"

I had always supposed Old Man Meany was in his old age already, but apparently it was something he was still looking forward to.

"Okay," I said. "I get it. Take it out and stuff it in your pockets. Stuff it in my pockets. I won't steal it, I promise."

"You don't understand," groaned Means. "It's all over. The foot . . . the head . . . the middle. I'd never know when I had it all."

It did seem to me that if you had to be cracked enough to keep your money in a mattress instead of putting it in the bank, you might at least put it all in one part of the mattress, tied up in a neat bundle. But I suppose that would tend to make the mattress lumpy. Anyhow, there seemed to be only one thing to do. I started to roll the mattress, yelling at Means to get a rope to tie it with.

As soon as he saw I was going to do what he wanted, he was all sweetness and light.

"A rope? Of course! Right away! Down in the cellar—no, of course, I moved everything out of the cellar. In the kitchen. . . ."

He stopped talking as he opened the door to the stairs. A swishing noise came up from below. It sounded awfully near.

"I'm afraid any rope I have is in the kitchen . . . that is, was in the kitchen. That's the one thing I didn't bring upstairs."

I thought fast. A mattress is an awkward thing to move. Without rolling it, it would be impossible.

"How about a belt? What you hold your pants up with—give it here quick!"

I had the mattress rolled now. One pull on a belt and I could heave it out the window and push Means after it and goodby to this rattrap. And then I remembered what Old Meany looked like. Even in the darkness I realized that his anatomy was not one that lends itself to wearing a belt. It would take more than that to keep his trousers from sliding down the inclined plane he used for a stomach. Old Man Meany wore suspenders.

"Never mind," I said. "You've got a sheet. Tear it up and hurry!"

We trussed up the mattress with strips of sheet

and I got ready to throw it into the boat. Mr. Mahoney ran the flashlight over it in astonishment.

"What's that?" he demanded. "What's taking so long?"

"Has the old man fainted?" Hank asked when he saw the mattress.

I heaved it toward his end of the boat. "Catch!" I told him. "And take good care of it. To Mr. Means, it's like a '32 Ford. All his money goes into it."

After that it was easy to get the old man out the window. In fact, he was in a great hurry to follow his mattress and I sure was in a hurry to follow him.

I don't know if Mr. Mahoney ever did figure it out. He said something to me later about the strange things people want to save in emergencies. I guess the picture of Old Man Meany clutching his mattress in the bottom of the boat was one he could never forget.

To my surprise, the old man didn't forget it either. When the waters had gone down and people began cleaning up the mess, he came to me and said he appreciated what I'd done for him that night. He knew the town was calling us hot-rodders heroes and stuff like that, but he wanted to do something concrete. He put his hand in his pocket and brought out one of those bills that I knew came from the mattress, and I saw I'd been right about their being big ones.

I thought of all the things I could buy with it, like a set of tires or a full race can or even a cutting torch. But then I thought of Mr. and Mrs. Mahoney and how they were having to give up the Waterview Stand because of all the damage and how we wouldn't have a place to meet anymore. So I told Mr. Means to give it to the Mahoneys or better yet to lend them a lot more so they could fix the place up and get on their feet again. He looked sort of unhappy at that and said he had his own place to fix up, if it could be fixed. And then I had an idea.

"Look, Mr. Means," I said. "You don't need to spend a cent on fixing up your place. The Library Ladies will do it for you. If you'd let them make it into a National Shrine, I'm sure they'd let you live there and all that. You could lend the Mahoneys the money you would have spent. That way there'll be two houses fixed instead of one."

"How do you know what the Library Ladies would do?" he asked.

"My mom's one of them and I heard her say so. And she said that if it was made into a National Shrine, they could get the money for it from the State or the Federal Government."

"And then we'd be right back where we were before—with all the jalopies around!" he protested.

"Well, I did have something of the kind in mind. But it's a good idea, don't you think, Mr. Means?"

Old Man Meany put the bill back in his pocket. "I suppose it would be too much to expect," he said, "with all the things that river washed away, that it could get rid of that collection of jalopies!"

Then he went into the Waterview Stand to talk to the Mahoneys.

The Night the Clock
Struck Thirteen

◆━━◆━━◆━━◆━━◆

PATRICIA McCUNE

LAURIE Shenfield, hidden in the brown wing chair, her feet tucked under her tightly, peered around through the door of her father's study. She could see Rick Weston's profile and the back of Yung Gi Kim's head and she could hear her father's voice droning through its lecture. Oh, why didn't that silly English lesson end! There were better things to do on a Saturday afternoon. She and Rick had plans. But Rick always had to sit through Yung Gi's lessons. Four times a week it'd been, for the entire semester, while she'd sat in the brown wing chair waiting. Waiting. Waiting.

"Why do you always have to stay with him, with Yung Gi Kim?" she'd asked Rick a dozen times. "Can't he have his lessons alone? How come the head of the high school English department can't tutor English without you?"

But she knew it was Rick Weston who spoke Korean, not her father. When she saw Rick's frown, saw the lines spring deeply between his gray eyes, she felt a quick remorse for her words.

As usual, the remorse burned away swiftly, leaving the old resentments, the old feelings of being apart, separated, alone. Why did her father have to be the head English teacher anyway? It would've been different if he'd been a professor at the university. After all, they lived in a university town. From her bedroom window, Laurie could see the tall campanile standing as a sentinel on the campus quadrangle and the brick buildings scattered boldly among the eucalyptus on the grassy slopes.

The high school meant nothing. Nothing at all. And sooner or later everyone in high school had Mr. Shenfield for a teacher. Everyone. That was the miserable part. He could be so severe. Such a tough grader. Laurie knew he was unpopular. Her own father.

"Well, I guess that's it." Rick's deep voice startled her.

"You're finished early. How come? It's not like Dad to give up so soon." Laurie was on her feet in a minute.

"My finals start Monday," Yung Gi said.

"And we have three more weeks of school," Rick groaned. "You college guys have all the luck."

"I hope so," Yung Gi said and left them there.

"Rick, you mean no more English lessons? We have the summer to ourselves? Soon, I mean?"

Rick nodded and smiled and Laurie felt suddenly wonderful. Summers were always the best time of year. No school. No books. No studying. No lectures from her father. She could spend hours away from the rambling book-filled house with its musty academic cloud hanging heavily over her wherever she turned. Once school was out there'd be a hundred things to do.

And there were. But the first three days and nights after school was over, Laurie was forced to remain inside. Because of her final grades, Mr. Shenfield had explained. Mrs. Matthews, the housekeeper, crept around grudgingly serving dinner to both of them, her strange eyes averted but reproachful nevertheless, while Mr. Shenfield lectured.

"Laurie, why do you do it? Why do you deliberately fail—"

"I didn't fail!" Laurie felt the cutting of her own voice and turned her head in unconscious defense. "I passed all my courses."

"But Laurie, just barely. You can do so much better. You deliberately do as poorly as you can. I don't understand it. I honestly don't understand." Mr. Shenfield bent his head and stared at his dinner without speaking again and Laurie felt her throat tighten in the remorse that assailed her.

"I'm sorry, Dad. I'm sorry about my bad grades.

I'll try to do better." But as she spoke Laurie knew it was summer and she'd have weeks and weeks of freedom before the necessity of studying would descend upon her again.

On the fourth night after school had closed, Laurie's punishment ended. Rick came to chicken dinner and afterwards they walked to the village theater.

It was a glorious time, even though the stars were veiled behind the June night mist, and the quarter moon was lost in the vast gray sky. It was glorious even though the double feature had been tiresome and the village malt shop bulging with students. It was enough to be with Rick again, the long summer stretching languidly before them.

It was almost midnight when they reached the cypress hedge at the corner of Laurie's street and the clock in the village tower would soon begin the long toll. They'd better hurry. She didn't relish any more punishment.

But there'd been time to spare. Laurie was in her room when the chimes rang clearly in the still night. She counted softly with them. "One, two, three . . . eight, nine . . . ten, eleven, twelve."

Then into the night, toneless in its imitation, muted and unheralded, throbbed the thirteenth chord.

"My gosh! It rang thirteen times!" Laurie's words pressed out through the back of her hand which had flung involuntarily against her mouth. Maybe it

112

was an echo, she thought. Probably the mechanism went haywire.

In a moment, the silent village was alive again. Students emerged from the malt shop. Lights filled windows. Without thinking, Laurie raced out of the house, heading automatically toward the village center where the clock tower stood staunchly. "After him!" someone yelled, as a shrouded figure skimmed off across the village square and out of sight in the gray mist.

"My gosh," Laurie whispered.

"It looked like a ghost," someone breathed beside her. "He must have accidentally done something to the clock to cause that thirteenth bong. I'm sure he didn't mean to have the whole town chase after him."

"Do you think they'll catch him?" Laurie asked, but no one answered her.

They didn't catch him. All anybody found was a thin white cotton blanket. "He had this wrapped around him," one summer student said. "All the better to be a ghost, I guess. But he's disappeared now. Could be any one of us here for all the evidence we have."

"Where'd the blanket come from?" a girl in the crowd asked.

No one knew.

But Laurie'd recognized it in a minute by the way Mrs. Matthews had mended one of the corners. It was a Shenfield blanket, all right, but Laurie couldn't claim it. Couldn't own up to it there in the village square in front of everyone. It made her sick. When she saw Rick come out of the shadows she was so relieved only a vague curiosity about where he'd been stirred in the corners of her mind.

"Rick, take me home."

"Sure. The ghost won't be back here tonight, anyway."

"Don't call it a ghost."

"Why not?"

"Because there's no such thing."

"Well, it looked like one. And by morning everybody in town will be calling it one. 'The ghost,' they'll say. 'Let's go hunt for the ghost.' And we'll probably all be out looking every night."

Laurie thought of the white cotton blanket and shivered. "I can think of better things to do."

"You're awfully jumpy all of a sudden," Rick said. "You scared?"

Why not, Laurie thought, when the town ghost is shrouded in one of your own blankets? Laurie supposed it'd be easy enough to steal the blanket from the clothesline, but Mrs. Matthews would've complained of that. Certainly Mrs. Matthews was not the ghost. Or was she? She was weird enough, Laurie thought, with those amber eyes and hair to match. Laurie could clearly remember the day Mrs. Matthews chased her all over the house with a broom—for no reason. It'd be just like Mrs. Mat-

114

thews to be a ghost—for no reason. Except to embarrass Mr. Shenfield, maybe.

Of course Mr. Shenfield was home with his books preparing tomorrow's lessons for the new summer students. Laurie couldn't remember when there weren't students filing in and out of her father's study for special lessons. Undoubtedly he was home. For a moment Laurie's mind froze, refusing to relinquish a terrifying thought. Could her father have used the white cotton blanket tonight? Could he possibly be the ghost? Was he really home now?

Laurie could feel the warmth draw from her face and she forced her mind, painstakingly, to accept the knowledge that her father was home in his study with his books. Her thoughts lightened with the comforting truth and she smiled briefly. Why did her mind play such tricks? Of all people in the whole town, why would she think of her own father as the ghost? Because of a blanket? What a foolish quirk of judgment.

But when Laurie and Rick reached the house, Mr. Shenfield was not at home. Laurie raced to the study. There was no one there. She called but there was no answer. Small twists of panic paralyzed her and she wondered why her mind insisted on tormenting her. Why should her father—

"Rick, what're we going to do?"

"Don't worry. Your dad's probably out chasing the ghost. Having a little excitement for a change."

"But—"

"But what?"

"Nothing. Nothing. See you tomorrow?"

"Sure. See you tomorrow."

After Rick left, Laurie sat down rigidly in the brown wing chair to wait.

The summer's debut was hardly auspicious, Laurie thought all the next morning. The first few school-less days had fallen far below her expectations. Now tonight, of all silly things, was "ghost night." It hadn't taken the college students long to organize everyone. They'd planned a big party to scour the countryside in search of the ghost. Some fun.

"And what do they plan to do with him when they catch him?" Laurie asked Rick after he'd given her the news.

"Well, golly, Laurie, we've got to catch him. Even if we don't know what to do with him yet. We can't just let a ghost go around loose."

"Why not? He's not hurting anyone. Maybe there's an explanation."

"Okay, so when we catch him, we'll ask him."

"Well, I'm not going."

"Laurie!"

"I mean it."

"What're you afraid of? If you think I'm not protection enough for you, there'll be dozens of others along. Older guys. Al Hanna's going along. You always went for him."

Laurie felt the hurt in his voice, the disbelief, the faint remnants of hope. "That's not the reason. I'm just not going. By the way, Al cancelled his lesson with Dad today."

"Why'd he do that?"

"How should I know?"

"Well, I don't like him. Always trying to be funny. Playing jokes all the time that are about as clever as a—as a ghost in the village clock tower. I never could understand what you see in him."

"Rick, you make me mad."

"Well, why don't you come with us tonight?"

"For the last time. I'm not going."

Even though Laurie tried to be disgusted and wanted to be indifferent, she knew it was little jabs of fear that had pricked at her all day. Her father had come home last night so flushed, so breathless, so silent. He wouldn't talk. Wouldn't say a word. This morning, she'd discovered the other white cotton blanket missing from the linen closet. How could she tell Rick? She wouldn't go out hunting for the ghost no matter what Rick said.

"A whole gang of us are going, Laurie. It'll be fun. What's wrong with you, anyway?"

"I don't want to go."

Rick stood stiffly for a moment, then turned abruptly, marching from the house without another word.

Laurie wanted desperately to call out to him, to confide her worries, but words choked in her throat. Only her arms stretched out as if to bring him back, but he didn't see. When the front door slammed behind him, she retreated to the brown wing chair, where her brooding was uninterrupted until Mrs. Matthews announced that dinner was almost ready. Laurie'd had half a notion to ask Mrs. Matthews about the blanket.

"You'd better set the table, Laurie," Mrs. Matthews said, "and stop moping. You've been sitting in that chair all afternoon. You have a squabble with Rick?"

"Not exactly." Laurie jumped up quickly so Mrs. Matthews would not pursue the questioning, and helped more than usual to prove her good spirits. The tactic stopped Mrs. Matthews's probing, but not Mr. Shenfield's.

"Why all the sudden cooperation?" her father asked at dinner. "Are you afraid I won't allow you to join the ghost searchers tonight?"

Always it came back to her father. Laurie could feel her body electrify with his question. Her fingers tightened around her fork and her hand remained immobile midway between her plate and her mouth. She knew his casual overtones were cover for a deeper seriousness. She knew him that well.

"I didn't think I'd go tonight."

"Your punishment's over, Laurie. Won't it look strange if you're the only one in the crowd not at the hunt?"

"They won't miss me."

"Not even Rick?"

At the mention of Rick's name, Laurie drew in her breath slowly, attempting to conceal the churning inside her. "Do you think it's a good idea for me to go tonight?" she asked testily, ignoring the reference to Rick. The conversation was moving too fast in a direction she couldn't control, but Laurie knew she couldn't talk about Rick right now.

"If you mean, do I think it's dangerous, I'm sure no one will see the ghost tonight."

"You're sure? How can you be so sure?" Laurie realized her voice was pitched too high and she spoke too excitedly. "I mean—why do you think they won't find the ghost?"

"Well, if you were the ghost wouldn't you remain hidden while the whole world was in pursuit?"

Laurie tried to look at her father, but her vision was locked in a vacant stare while her mind repeated his words. Was he trying to tell her? The question that never abandoned her thoughts was the reason behind his behavior. She expected Mrs. Matthews to act queerly, but not her father. Had he been working too hard? Had there been too many students to tutor privately in addition to his regular classes? Too many like Al Hanna who'd decide suddenly not to come after a lesson had been planned? Laurie didn't know. She wanted to cry and she couldn't choke down any more of her dinner.

"Dad, will you excuse me? I don't feel very well." She almost ran from the table.

"I'll be in the study, if you want me, Laurie," Mr. Shenfield called after her.

Oh sure, he'd be in his study. He'd remain hidden while the whole world was in pursuit. That's what he'd said.

Laurie fell on her bed in a torment of exhaustion and fear. How long she lay there she wasn't aware, but when she finally stirred, she knew she'd been asleep a long time.

She lay quietly in the darkened bedroom, listening, thinking, hoping. Wondering what to do. Calmer, if only in the knowledge that the ghost was safe for one more night. The town was silent now. The luminous clock indicated two-thirty in the morning. The search would be over.

Laurie crept to the window, looking through the night. Her mind slipped automatically into anxiety as she became fully awake, her eyes darting from one obscure shadow to another outside her window. Only the campanile on the campus stood tall and clear, piercing the web of night like a missile prepared to blast-off. Well, not quite like a missile, Laurie thought, almost smiling through her worry. The old brick bell-tower, even with the bell removed, was really from another age.

Laurie liked the campanile and admired it in the nebulous light, wondering vaguely and irrelevantly if she'd ever set foot on the college campus as a student. Probably not, with her barely passing marks. She shrugged instinctively in the old habit and as she started to turn from the window caught sight with the edge of her eye of the mysterious phantom high in the campanile.

"My gosh!" She pressed against the pane with renewed excitement, at the top of her mind the gratifying news that the ghost was in the campanile and her father was asleep in his bedroom.

The specter floated at the tower windows briefly and then disappeared. "If he's leaving the campanile," Laurie said to herself, "I'll check his direction before I call—before I call Dad." But the shadows were too dark at the base of the campanile and Laurie didn't see the ghost again. "If he's still up there—maybe we—"

When Laurie cleared her mind of her father's guilt, she realized she'd also removed him as a possible searching partner. "I could never wake him now to go after a ghost," she said, needing Rick, admitting she'd never be brave enough to go alone. She looked at the clock on the night table again, wondering if she could telephone Rick at this hour. Losing valuable time vexed her. My gosh, the whole town'd been out after the ghost and she, Laurie Shenfield, had spotted him all by herself and couldn't do a thing about it!

As she groped for action, Laurie heard faint steps approaching, muted at first by the cypress hedge on the corner, the definite heel-to-pavement thumps becoming more distinct as they neared the Shenfield house. They turned finally, at the front gate, and in one sickening moment, Laurie recognized her father. He hadn't been asleep! He'd been out roaming—after the whole world had given up the pursuit—

"Oh, Dad!" Laurie's cry was muffled in the palms of her hands as she sank to her bed, defeated and alone.

In the morning, Laurie's muscles ached and her arms were numb. Her position hadn't changed since she'd collapsed on the bed. She wondered how she could have fallen asleep with her last thoughts so anguished. "And what do I do now?" she said aloud, knowing she'd have to call Rick. That is, if he'd speak to her. Well, the sooner she found out, the better, she decided, dashing to the telephone in a whirl of sudden action.

"Rick, about last night—" Laurie, her heart pounding in relief, could tell in a minute he was glad she'd called.

"It's okay, Laurie. We didn't find the spook anyway. We probably scared him off."

"That's what Dad said would happen." She paused. "But Rick—"

"Yeah, Laurie."

"The reason I stayed home. I can't tell you about it over the 'phone. Will you come over? Right away?"

"Sure. Be there in ten minutes."

When Rick arrived, Laurie, painfully close to tears, made several faltering attempts to tell her story. Finally, Rick gripped her shoulders and shook her gently. "Come on, now. It can't be that bad."

"It is, Rick. It's awful."

"It's about the ghost. I can tell that much."

Laurie nodded.

"You know who it is? You have some information?" Rick wheedled the report from her slowly, carefully.

"The blanket, Rick. Remember the white cotton blanket? Remember how it was mended in the corner?"

"I remember the blanket. You know whose it is?"

Laurie nodded again and took a deep breath. "It's ours. Right out of our linen closet. Rick, another like it is missing. I don't know what to do."

When Rick didn't answer, Laurie went on. "The worst of it is, I think——" she stopped, unable to continue.

"Go on, Laurie. Go on."

"Well, it's Dad. I think——I think he's the ghost. I don't know why he should be, but I'm afraid he is."

"Laurie, you can't mean that. Not seriously. Why he'd be the last man—— There's no reason."

She told him the rest of her story, then. Mr. Shenfield's strange behavior. Their conversations. His disappearances. Seeing the ghost in the campanile last night.

"Laurie, we checked the campanile. There was no ghost in the campanile last night."

"There was about two-thirty this morning. I saw him from my bedroom window. And then Dad came home a little later. I saw that, too. Rick, what're we going to do?"

"I don't know. I think we'll have to catch the ghost ourselves. Alone. The two of us. No other guys."

"Just us?" Laurie's excitement showed in her voice at first, but subsided quickly. "Rick, how can I catch my own father? That's impossible."

"I don't think we'll catch your father. But even if we do—well, Laurie, you can't go on this way. It's got to be settled. We'll find out his reasons."

Laurie was quiet. She looked at Rick and he took her hand.

"It isn't your father, Laurie."

How can he be so positive, Laurie wondered, adding quickly, "When do we go on this—this ghost hunt?"

"Tonight. Late. After midnight."

"How'll I get out of the house?"

"You'll have to sneak out."

"I suppose if Dad's out roaming around, it'll be

124

easy enough. Mrs. Matthews'll never hear me. Maybe she roams, too."

"It's all settled then. I'll figure out the details by tonight."

Their search began shortly after the village clock struck twelve. Laurie noticed particularly there were only twelve strikes. "That's one place we won't have to look," she said as she met Rick at the front gate.

"Where's that?"

"The village clock tower. I'll bet once in there was enough for him."

"We're headed for the campanile, Laurie. Was your dad asleep?"

"How can you sneak out of a house without anyone knowing if you open doors all over the place?" She didn't mean to be cross, but she truly didn't know whether her father was in his room or not.

The world seemed to close in on them as they passed the cypress hedge at the corner. It was a black night. No moon. Laurie could feel the damp touch of air on her face and a chill shimmied up her spine.

"Scared, Laurie?"

"A little." She held his hand tighter. "Just don't leave me alone." After all, Rick was tall and strong. He—

"Shh." Rick stopped short and pulled Laurie close to the bushes. "Once we cross this street we have no protection," he whispered. "Let's take a good look now and head fast for the campanile."

Was Rick planning to go up inside the campanile? Were they going to walk right smack into the ghost with no means of escape except the very steps they'd climbed? There were no lights. The staircase was ancient and worn and unsteady.

"Rick, just because I saw him there last night doesn't mean anything. Don't you think we should do some more searching before we concentrate on the campanile?" Laurie could feel her fear returning. Short little jabs of it that caught at her breath.

"We know he was up in the village clock tower and we know he was up in the campanile. At least you said you saw him last night. He probably likes to be up high. And the campanile doesn't have any clock mechanism to run into." He pulled Laurie after him across the slippery grass.

"Did you bring your flashlight, Rick?"

"Yeah, but I don't see how we can use it. We don't want him to know we're here until it's too late for him to act."

"You have the rope?"

"Yeah, but here, you keep it. Don't talk any more, Laurie. We've got to concentrate from now on."

In another minute they were at the base of the campanile and Laurie ran her fingers over the rough bricks, feeling for the entrance, following Rick inside when the heavy door gave slowly under pressure. The staircase was immediately before them and they began the circular climb single file, the steps creaking ominously, the flimsy banister yielding to the weight of their arms, forcing Laurie to lean to the wall for support. It was almost dank inside the brick shaft, tomb-like, smelling of old air. Laurie could understand why the ghost would need a blanket, even a thin one.

Three-quarterway up the steps, Laurie stumbled, crying out automatically as she sprawled across the spiral stairs, frozen there in sudden panic.

In an instant all was still again. Rick grabbed her arm to steady her, then they maneuvered the last half dozen steps on hands and knees. When they finally reached the narrow wooden landing at the top of the bell-less tower, Laurie, in one long thin sigh, released the breath she'd been holding, and with her heart beating wildly, helped Rick grope across the rough boards for the ghost.

There was no ghost in the campanile.

Had Rick known all along there wouldn't be? Is that why—could Rick be— The sinister thought twisted through her and in a sudden compulsion she broke the eerie silence. "I'm sorry I cried out," she said, trying to see Rick in the dark, to discern his form in the opaque night.

Icy fear edged in on her as she recalled Rick the night of the thirteenth chime, the way he'd slipped in from the shadows. At the time she'd thought he'd been chasing the ghost, but— "Oh, Rick."

"Don't worry. There's no ghost here so it didn't make any difference that you called out." Laurie detected the disappointment in his voice and couldn't help feeling relieved. Rick was not the ghost and that was all there was to it. He beamed the flashlight, moving his arm back and forth rapidly at first, then slackening as the light verified an empty campanile.

"What do we do next?" she asked, hope returning.

"We wait."

"Here?" She began to suspect the reason Rick hadn't told her the details of their hunt. It was too late now to argue with him.

"Yeah, here. I think this is where he hangs out and I'm sure he won't be expecting our surprise party."

"Rick. Don't hurt him. Just in case—" Her mind was back on her father again.

They stopped talking then and waited. Laurie spent so much time waiting. Always waiting.

Occasionally, Rick stood up to peer out the window, careful to remain hidden from view, but he didn't see the ghost coming. It was Laurie who heard the heavy door opening below them. She clutched Rick's ankle and he dropped beside her.

The phantom ascended the spiral staircase slowly. Laurie could see the faint blob of white against the ebony night. Small shocks of fear assailed her,

her muscles tensing with it. She held her breath and waited the long slow wait while the ghost circled higher and higher.

Then, as if sensing the unusual, the ghost halted midway. While Laurie exhaled on a long breath, her fists clenched tightly, the ghost turned and began a hurried descent. Instantaneously, Rick was on his feet. "Light," he yelled and plunged down the rickety steps three at a time as Laurie grabbed the flashlight and sent a yellow glow after him.

She followed quickly, but Rick had chased the ghost half way across the slippery grass and stopped him with a flying tackle before she caught up to them and held the light unsteadily on the ghost's face.

"Yung Gi Kim," she said softly, and sank to the ground on her knees beside them. "Yung Gi, how come? What're you doing? I don't understand." Knowledge eased into the back of her mind that the ghost was not her father, spreading the relief through her body, but seeing Yung Gi was a new shock and questions spilled out of her mouth in confusion.

Yung Gi answered in a flood of Korean, and Rick took up the questioning. While Yung Gi continued his torrent of words, Rick looked at Laurie quietly. "He flunked out of college. He had to leave the dorm and he couldn't go home. He'd lose face if he went home. He's the eldest son."

As Yung Gi babbled incoherently, Laurie felt his fright, his panic. Obviously, he hadn't planned to be a ghost. It was all because of that accidental thirteenth chime of the village clock. The students and townspeople had taken it from there. But could a person feel so strongly about school and passing marks that he'd have to—have to—

"Yung Gi, is it that important?" She thought of her own poor marks and her lack of interest and tried to understand this student who could not face his own family with his failure. She'd certainly faced her own father often enough with poor marks. Watching Yung Gi, seeing his torment, Laurie felt an unexplained shame of her own school record and lack of concern. Her father'd begged her to be more serious and why hadn't she? Why had she deliberately defied him? At least Yung Gi had tried. She hadn't even tried.

She leaned back on her heels in sudden remorse. Was it all because her dad taught at her school and she wished he didn't? Her remorse did not lessen in its usual pattern, but stayed with her until she knew a small resolve had taken form, knowing it never would have without the ghost. Suddenly, she wanted to help Yung Gi; do something to get him back in school where he wanted to be. Somehow make up for all her own failures.

"Rick, did he fail because he doesn't know English well enough?"

130

"He says so."

"Why don't we help him? I know all about English." When Rick laughed, Laurie couldn't speak for a moment. Why, even Rick thought of her as a poor student. And that wasn't it at all. "Well, I mean it, Rick. You can just stop laughing."

In their loquacity, they hadn't heard Mr. Shenfield approach. They didn't see him in the graying light until he stood above them on the grass, his own flashlight fixed on them. "Laurie!" His voice rang out in the still night.

"Dad? Dad, we caught the ghost. It's Yung Gi Kim. We're going to help him, Dad. Please?" Laurie jumped to her feet. "We don't want to tell anyone. Do we have to?" She paused, looking at her father questioningly. "What are you doing here?" she asked abruptly.

Mr. Shenfield smiled. "I've been looking for Yung Gi."

"You knew?" Laurie was incredulous.

"I suspected. That's all. I knew he'd failed. When he disappeared, I suspected."

"And you want to help?" Laurie was hopeful.

"I want to help," Mr. Shenfield said.

"And we won't have to tell anyone?"

"No," Mr. Shenfield said. "The college students can go on having ghost night for years. The ghost story will get better and better. The campus will get more and more haunted. But no one will ever find the ghost. Now come on, let's all go home before someone sees us." Mr. Shenfield put his arm around Laurie's shoulder and the four of them walked back to the house together.

To Fly a Plane

KAY HAUGAARD

THE little silver, two seater plane bobbed as it hit another air pocket. It rose in a bucking motion over the dark timberland. Margo Eckhert looked away from her father's intent profile and peered out the window. She searched the sea of trees for a little brown square. It would be the landing field for the town of Junction, her destination for the summer.

The plane jerked again. Margo's red curls bobbed and her stomach flopped. But the thought of her first job waiting for her down there made her more uneasy than the motion of the plane. Her father's shoulders leaned into the bucking motion as he would have done on a bronco.

Looking down at her father's black cowboy

boots, Margo smiled. "Don't let 'er throw you, Dad. Keep that wheel straight." Then she reached toward the controls. "Here, let me show you how."

Her father turned his sun-tanned face toward her. "Just keep your little grubby paws off, Miss Know-It-All. I don't want you tinkering with my plane."

"But Daddy! Why won't you teach me to fly? I practically know how already from all the time I've spent flying with you and . . ." She was becoming excited. "I navigated when we flew over to Butte and Cheyenne and . . . and . . . you said yourself these new planes are as simple to fly as riding a bicycle." She sounded pouty, "Oh, Daddy, why won't you let me learn to fly?"

"You'd break your pretty little empty head." Her father shot a smile at her that brought out all the laugh wrinkles around his eyes. "Honey! You'd start thinking about what dress you were going to wear to the Hop or what Norma said to Thelma or if that 'Dee-vine boy' was going to ask you to have a coke with him. Sweetheart, when you fly a plane, you have to be serious!"

Margo didn't speak. Her father was probably right. She didn't really feel capable of flying. Maybe she only hoped she was capable of it. In fact there weren't many things Margo felt certain she could do. She didn't even know about the job at the Mill, for instance. Oh, it was nice of Mr. McAllister to think of her when he needed a bookkeeper but Margo wasn't fooled. She knew he was just doing it because he and her dad were such good friends.

She continued staring silently at the undulating masses of mountains below. The towering trees covering their rugged surfaces were reduced to a dark, black-green fuzz by the distance.

Suddenly she looked again. "Hey, Dad, better start dropping and banking north. There's the field."

Eckhert craned his head out over the side of the little plane, tipping it for a better look, then he started down in a wide, swooping arc. The engine cut and the high whine slid down the scale with the altitude, then caught and rose again momentarily as Eckhert brought it up smoothly to miss a ridge near the field. With a banking glide, he cut the engine again and touched ground, taking it down the runway in a solid three pointer. The sound changed to the "chucketa chucketa chucketa" of the slowing engine and the plane's vibration over the unpaved dirt runway. He slammed on the brakes, stopping neatly in line with McAllister's own plane; a different color, but otherwise the same plane.

"Pretty nice landing, hah?" Eckhert turned to his daughter for approval.

"Pretty nice, Dad. But you said yourself that a monkey could fly this plane. You know; no ground looping, no nose-over, no nothing!"

"All right, Miss Know-It-All. Next you are going

to try to convince me that you are as smart as a monkey and *that* will take some doing."

Eckhert threw open the door of the plane. As district representative for the Mutual Insurance Company for the past twenty-five years, Eckhert had met Mac, as he called McAllister, as his first big account. Mac owned a sawmill out in the Siskiyous and needed insurance. Eckhert was just the man to provide it. Over the years, the relationship grew from just business to a deep, personal friendship.

"How's Mr. McAllister's mill doing, Daddy?"

"That's the reason I took the trouble to fly you over rather than sending you on the train, Margo. I wanted to talk to Mac. He's been having kind of a rough time."

Margo started climbing out of the plane, hopping down on one foot, then extracting her second foot while hanging on the wing. She was in this awkward position when she heard a deep, masculine voice.

"Let me help you." And she was lifted down gently.

Margo turned around quickly, trying to push her hair back in place, pull her skirt down and straighten her sweater all at the same time. *What had Daddy said about a "dee-vine boy"? Well, here he is,* thought Margo. *Of course he's really a man. But on him it looks good!*

She looked away from his too direct smile.

136

He held out his hand to Eckhert. "I'm Brian Prentiss, sir. I'm second in command. But Mr. McAllister has gone to a hearing and I've moved up a notch for the day."

Brian drove them over to the McAllister home across from the office where Margo would work. On the short drive from the landing field, Brian told them something about the hearing going on in Junction.

"It's about logging for the National Forest." Brian's face was very serious. "We haven't got more than a few thousand we can log before something has to be done. Mr. McAllister has been negotiating with the Federal Government to be able to log some of the National Forest area, but who knows how it will come out? If they decide he can't, it might be the end of the mill and that would ruin Mr. McAllister."

Eckhert spoke quietly. "All that money he's been pouring into this insurance year after year. Seems a pity it can't help him out somehow."

During the next week Margo was busy getting acquainted with the office routine and the area. She had her own room over the garage by the McAllisters. It was certainly a different world; a womanless one. She and Mrs. Mac were the only women on the place. But there were only a few of the men that she came in contact with. Other than Mr. McAllister and Brian, there was Big Louis, a beefy man in heavy, high laced boots who was chief sawyer. He had only had the job a short while, since Old Tony had been turned out to pasture. Old Tony had been around for so long that when it came time to retire him, Mr. McAllister didn't have heart to let him go entirely. So Tony became yard and light maintenance man.

Margo was on her way over to the McAllisters' for Sunday dinner when she saw Old Tony digging around the rhododendrons. His blue faded overalls hung out from his thin chest in a big, hammock-like billow as he leaned over the dark earth.

"Hi, Tony." Margo raised her hand to him as she walked up the board steps.

"Hello, Miss Eckhert. How's the office coming? How do you like it here?"

"Fine, Tony. It's fun to be up here in the mountains."

"Yeah, it's all right, I guess. But don't hang around too long. They'll have you scrubbing floors and washing windows."

Margo was startled. "What makes you say that?"

"Look at me! They think I'm too old to be sawyer anymore so they give me this." He jammed the ground viciously with the trowel. "Woman's work, that's what this is . . . growing pretty flowers. I'm still a better man than that blockhead they've got now. He hasn't the brains of a pine stump."

Margo just kept walking up the steps to the house. She smiled because she didn't take Old Tony seriously. No one did. He was always griping. It was just Tony.

"Oh, now, Tony. No woman could make those rhododendrons bloom the way you have. They are all in love with you."

He looked up and stopped frowning for a moment in what was as near as he seemed able to come to a smile.

Brian's desk was back quite a way from Margo's but he didn't seem to mind walking the distance several times a day to the water fountain in front.

In fact, it was only the third day she was there that Brian presented himself before her desk.

"How about a little jeep ride to Sunset Point after work?"

So they went for a jeep ride. The next day it was a picnic up by Panther Rock and the day after it was a walk to the Great Tree.

As they walked along the spongy forest path between straight-trunked, high-limbed firs and the moist greenness of sword fern, Brian told her a lot about himself.

"Yup, I've done about every job here on the place. Started out as errand boy; then a short stint as truck driver. Then I worked in the mill, pulling a green chain, part sawyer, bucking boards . . . you know . . . everything."

He told of how McAllister had gradually let him in on the operation and management of the whole enterprise. He had spent his evenings studying saw-mill operation; poring over lumbermen's texts and publications.

Brian turned to look at Margo. "And all the time McAllister was telling me what a big future was in store for me; how I'd take over the place someday." He raised his hands slightly, palms out in a kind of shrug. "So here I am, right next to the top."

"You're so young for such a position too!" Margo was filled with admiration.

"Now I have a feeling that McAllister is going to come back from those hearings and say, 'Son, here's the sack. Climb in and go jump in Bullseye Lake.' "

"Mr. McAllister wouldn't say that!"

Brian was solemn as he poked the browned lay-ers of fir needles with his boot. "No," he seemed cool and distant. "You're right, he wouldn't say it that way." He laughed. "Oh, well, I've always wanted to work for some little pecker wood outfit."

"It's too bad." Margo was thoughtful. "But you can still learn to do a dozen other things if you want to."

"I guess you're right, Blue Eyes." Brian smiled at Margo as though he had just met her only that moment and was pleased with what he saw.

The hearings continued through July and into August. August sixth was the day of decision. When McAllister came back that day he didn't have to tell anyone what the results were.

He came striding into the office in the dark green lumberman's jacket and trousers that had been his uniform for nearly thirty years. As he walked he studied the floor. Coming to his desk, he sat down without greeting anyone. He stared at the picture on his desk of Mrs. Mac and his two boys. Or was he just focusing on nothingness and the picture happened to be in the direction he was facing?

No one spoke to him. No one needed to. Now and then Margo would glance in through the semi-partition and see him still sitting there, rocking from side to side in his swivel chair with his hands folded over his stomach or just running his hand through the gray blond of his thinning hair.

Of course he did tell everyone soon after. The next day to be exact. After Brian's talk with McAllister he walked right by Margo's desk without even looking up.

Watching him pass, Margo didn't know for whom she felt most sorry, Brian or Mr. McAllister.

The day Mrs. Mac went to visit her sister in Red Bluff it happened. It was Saturday afternoon. Brian had gone to Junction in the company car on business. The other men had loaded in the truck and gone too, to spend their paychecks of the night before. The place was almost deserted. There was a general air of depression about the place.

Margo was glad that her father had called to say he would be flying over the mill on his way to Beaver Marsh Hunting Lodge, and might as well drop down for an hour or so.

"Besides, Hon," he had said, over the phone. "I'm worried about how Mac is taking all this. I've got a few things I want to talk to him about."

Now, as she walked through the empty, silent yard on her way to the office, the strange loneliness of the atmosphere seemed a foreboding of the mill's coming demise. It was almost as though it was already a collection of dead, empty buildings.

She looked up to see Old Tony mowing the lawn in front of the McAllister residence.

"Hi, Tony," Margo walked across the dirt road. "Why aren't you in town spending your money with the others?"

"Me?" He looked up from the lawnmower for a moment, leaning on the handle. "Money? What money? I've given practically my whole life for this crumby outfit and now what happens. They are going to turn me off."

"Everyone has to leave, Tony, even Mr. McAllister. The whole place is folding."

He started pushing the lawnmower again. "I can tell you sure, it isn't mowing the lawn I feel like doing."

142

"What do you mean, Tony?"

"Just you never mind what I mean." He turned and started mowing away from her.

Margo could hardly keep her mind on making out the quarterly returns that morning. It was too quiet with just her and Mr. McAllister. Besides, she was looking forward to seeing her father. The time went slowly.

Her father came in right on schedule. It was good to see him again and get news from home. The three of them went down by the log pond to eat their lunch. It was very pleasant, except for the vague way poor Mr. McAllister acted. Eckhert tried what he could, in his own bluff way, to buck him up. Finally, Margo could sense that the two men wanted to speak alone. She rose from the grass and said, "I think I'll wander back and get those returns finished."

The men were so deep in conversation they just nodded acknowledgment and her father said, "All right, sweetheart. I'll see you."

"You going to leave for Beaver Marsh right away, Dad?"

"Afraid I'll have to, Hon." He gave a perfunctory smile.

She went back to her desk. The returns only took about an hour then she went out into the yard to stretch her legs and see if Mr. McAllister and Dad were still talking. She thought she'd exchange a few words with Old Tony too on her way by the house but he was gone. Everyone was gone. Her father and Mr. McAllister were no longer by the Mill Pond. Then she heard a roar in the distance. It was her father's plane taking off.

Then she saw it! For a couple of moments she just stared stupidly at the corner of the storage shed next to the main building. It was releasing a thin tendril of smoke that writhed and reached and stretched toward the blue sky.

Running quickly to the door of the building she saw the leaping flames were roof high inside the building, crackling the dry wood hungrily. And there, before the raging fire, was the figure of a man standing immobile and transfixed.

It was Mr. McAllister. The expression on his face was distant, as though he had been stunned and had withdrawn into himself.

"Mr. McAllister! Why don't you call the forest service! Call them, quick!"

The blank face behind the glasses did not speak. It only shook back and forth slowly. Margo grabbed him by the arm and led him from the burning shed. She had to give a little jerk to his arm several times. He seemed reluctant to move from the sight. Once he was outside safely, she left him and ran to the office to telephone the forest service. What had made Mr. McAllister do it?

As she picked up the receiver to dial she noticed that the cord had been cut and was dangling by the side of the desk. The emotional strain of losing the hearing must have been the final blow. How logical to burn the mill and then collect the insurance. He would be able to live comfortably the rest of his life on two hundred thousand.

But even as she saw the incriminating evidence Margo could not believe it.

As she glanced around the office she noticed that Mr. McAllister's desk was strewn carelessly with papers and the cash box was gone. The papers looked important, but she didn't have time to play detective. She had to report that fire. Where had Old Tony gone anyway at this crucial moment? If only Brian and the men would return, they could drive to Junction to tell the forest service. If the fire wasn't put out quickly, not only the mill and the surrounding buildings would be demolished but who knows how many acres it would take if it ever got loose in the forest like a raging beast, glutting itself on forest growth, shacks and wildfire.

Margo rushed out of the office and caught a horrified view of the now towering blaze, licking and crackling skyward. Then she remembered Mr. McAllister. He was nowhere to be seen. She looked around wildly for someone else; anyone.

Then she saw a man waving to her from the distance. It was Brian and he was running toward her.

"That crazy fool McAllister has set fire to the mill." He grabbed Margo by the arm. "Come with me. I can't leave you here. I'm going to take the plane to Junction. It's the quickest way."

"I thought you went to Junction for the day," Margo managed to gasp between swallows of stinging air.

"I got done early and thought I might as well come back. Good thing I did."

"But where's McAllister?"

"Probably made his getaway somehow. Who knows?"

Margo scrambled into the little plane. Brian climbed in the opposite side. Soon he had the prop going and was bumping down the runway and then they were air borne.

"It's not even fifty miles air distance, we'll be there in no time." Margo spoke in a kind of daze, as though to herself. "I can't understand Mr. McAllister setting fire to the mill. It just isn't like him to be dishonest."

"Oh?" Brian raised his eyebrows skeptically. "The old buzzard just saw a good thing and couldn't resist it. After all, two hundred thousand will buy a lot of lollipops."

"But he was such a nice man. What makes you so sure?"

"Well, maybe I shouldn't be saying this, but only yesterday Old Tony was saying that Mr. McAllister

146

had said to him, 'If I was smart I'd just put a match to the whole thing.' "

"Old Tony said that?"

"Yup."

Margo's eyes were suddenly wide. "You know, I'll bet *he* did it. There's something funny about the way he disappeared just when the fire started." She thought of Old Tony's bitterness and shook her head sadly. It figured. That's probably when he came in the office and took the money, she told herself, while I was out eating lunch.

"It was the old buzzard himself, all right."

"What makes you so . . . so . . ." Margo sniffed the air with concern. "I smell gasoline."

"Must be your imagination." Brian clung to the wheel as the little plane rose and fell sharply.

"No, it isn't. I know. It's so close." Margo looked around for the gasoline then looked out the window onto the undulating expanse of dark green and spotted the railroad, stretching like a gleaming strand of wire twisting across and through the mountains to an opening in the trees with a couple gray box-like buildings. Their tin roofs winked in the sun.

Margo pointed to the railroad. "Hey, the iron compass says you are going the wrong direction to get to Junction. Better pull the nose over that way." Then, continuing to look for the leak, Margo glanced around the plane and over the back seat.

There, behind the seat, was the olive green metal cash box Mr. McAllister had kept his money in, so trustingly, right in the office.

"Hey, look back here. Here's the cash box!" She looked up at Brian.

"Had it all figured, didn't he? Guess we beat him to the plane before he had a chance."

"I . . . I . . . just can't believe . . ." Then Margo saw the source of the gasoline odor. The cuff of Brian's left pants leg was soaked. Without even thinking she said, "There, there, I knew I smelled gasoline. Say, how did it get on . . ." Then she stopped in mid sentence filled with horror and her eyes rose slowly to meet Brian's.

He was calm. His milky face was smooth and un-expressive. Then his blue eyes seemed almost to laugh before he said, "Yes, it was me all right. The old buzzard promised me a big, successful job. If he thinks he can turn me out with a lousy couple weeks' pay, I just hope he gets it along with the mill before they get there."

"You . . . you . . . passed the landing field." Margo pointed helplessly out the window toward a distant clearing.

"So I did. What do you know about that? And why shouldn't I? I have no interest in that world down there. I have everything in the world I want right here: a cash box full of money . . . and you." He smiled and put his hand over Margo's.

Margo felt her hands turn cold and numb. Then she withdrew them slowly.

"Don't say that. I'm not in on this thing. You're crazy. You can't do it."

"Yes we can, Blue Eyes, and we have enough in that box back there for a lot of goodies."

Margo's head was buzzing with rage and confusion. "You'll run out of gas. You don't know where you are going or how far the next field is." She made an unthinking, almost reflex lunge toward the controls but he grabbed her wrists and easily squeezed and twisted them until she let loose.

Brian looked at her coldly. "You know, Blue Eyes, if you aren't going to cooperate there's no need of keeping you around. Besides, I think this plane could do with a little less weight." He reached over and unlatched the door by Margo's side.

"No, no, no . . . you can't."

"You don't seem to think I can do anything."

Margo nearly fainted with fear as she caught a glimpse of the ground below, spiked with green swords of fir trees. Brian pushed the door open more and a wide margin of blue air came rushing in, wounding her with its freshness, snatching away even the flimsy security of the little plane. She felt unsupported in space. As the plane hit another air pocket, she crowded toward Brian, clutching his shirt; too frightened to even scream.

"Please, please." Margo found her voice. Then, as Brian pushed her away she grasped the seat

149

tightly with both hands, her finger tips turning white with the pressure of her fear and she screamed.

Then she stared at the cash box, the heavy, sharp-edged cash box behind the seat, with sudden recognition. Bracing her feet to keep from falling toward the open door, she reached back and grasped the box solidly with both hands.

Brian's hands were occupied with the door and the controls when she swung the heavy box back over her shoulders and, using all her strength and more than she ever dreamed she had, catapulted it overhand directly onto Brian's head.

He howled with anguish, writhing spasmodically, before slumping on the seat toward Margo.

Margo did not even have time to feel exultant over the triumph of the cash box when the little plane's engine cut and coughed and then started a slow, descending whine. It began nosing down, gradually.

She could hardly reach the controls over Brian's bulk sprawled over the seat. With a wrench of the same strength that had hurled the cash box, she freed herself from the weight of Brian's limp body, climbed over him to take the wheel firmly. With some shoving of his legs, she freed the pedals and began her frantic struggle to straighten the little plane. It was nosing down at a steeper and steeper angle and rapidly increasing speed. Even as she took the controls she saw the ground beginning to come at her in a big, slowly revolving pinwheel.

She felt panic grip her, felt it begin to blur her vision, then she thought of her father and willed his guiding hand into hers. *Pull 'er up, pull 'er up. Straighten that spin! Calm yourself, Honey, calm yourself.* Her hands stopped trembling and began working but the plane still headed down. Several seconds of horror lengthened into seeming hours by their intensity, before she was able to coordinate the nose and the wings to stop the spin. Then gradually the plane began to respond until, with a lurch and a buck, it nosed up into a slow ascent.

Margo sighed with a deepness that was painful and relaxed her grip. A slight smile came over her perspiring face and she reached over to tighten the latch on the door which still hung loose. Then she took a deep breath now that the plane was on a firm upward course. It was a cinch to keep it up there. She prayerfully breathed thanks that she had paid attention when she flew with her father.

As the plane cruised evenly she felt better. It was a good, stable feeling. For a moment she would just enjoy it before she started to worry about the next problem; landing.

She shoved Brian's arm a little farther out of interference range of the controls. He grimaced and groaned as she pushed and she felt a keen sense of relief that he was still alive. She would have to land quickly, before he gained consciousness. She would try to make it to Beaver Marsh Hunting Lodge where her father was.

She nosed the plane up so she could see wider and spot the open spaces. The ground below was a seemingly endless ocean of forest. It would be so reassuring if she could see the old iron compass somewhere. There had to be a railroad someplace. She pushed the little plane higher.

The compass on the control panel said she was going south. But was that good? Brian was blocking the map compartment and she couldn't remember exactly which direction Beaver Marsh was from Junction.

Scanning the ground she saw something; a round, blue, reflective area. Could it be Bullseye Lake? Of course it was! That was some help. Bullseye Lake was twenty miles east . . . or was it west from Beaver Marsh? Margo shook her head and it came to her with violent impact that *she* alone was flying the plane. Her father's hand was *not* beside her, ready to take over when she got tired, confused or panicky. *She* had to decide. Something told her it should be west so she didn't stop to think further but began banking wide. Her shoulder muscles were setting into tight knots and all she could think of were her father's words. "These new little birds with all the fancy controls are plenty easy to land but not so easy that you can't clobber yourself like Humpty Dumpty if you don't follow the rules."

She scanned the ground. Mile after mile of loathsome fir trees stood militantly guarding the precious ground.

Brian moaned and muttered in a semi-conscious stupor and rubbed his head.

The field! It was below, spread out like a great welcome mat. Like a sign of home and safety. Margo's stomach leaped to her mouth with illogical joy.

She began the approach descent slowly, the way she had seen her father do, making wide circles. Her hands were trembling. But it was so hard to judge. The ground came up so rapidly. She was going too fast. She eased up on the throttle, then it began to stall so she mounted skyward again after the unsuccessful attempt.

"Darn and double darn!" She hated herself for being so nervous. She hated the earth for tantalizing and teasing her. How she wanted to be down there. She cruised over the field once again trying to think her way out but catching a glimpse of the bobbling gas gauge, she came down again, closer, banking wide, close enough to see people coming out of the lodge down to one side of the field.

Every time she came down she realized how little the field really was and she couldn't seem to cut the speed. It would be suicide to try to land at that speed. *But it would be suicide not to.*

As she came down on her fourth attempt, Brian turned over and moved his arm out. She saw his eyelids flicker. She glanced at the speedometer with horror. The wheels hit the ground with a jolt that threw the controls from her and sent the plane careening down the little dirt field in a crazy, wobbling roll toward the fringe of fir trees around the perimeter. The ground was a gray blur streaking by. Brian half rose, half fell toward her so she couldn't reach the steering wheel to nose the plane away from the trees. But she managed to reach the brake and stomped on it with all her force. The plane slowed slightly but continued to hurtle toward the unyielding mass of trees. They were too close! Margo didn't even have time to brace herself before the plane hit the trees with a splintering sound.

And then there was stillness; absolute stillness holding her in its grasp for a wonderful, momentary eternity before the world came back to her in a rush of pain.

A man flung open the door and lifted her out. She was dazed and the pain in her leg . . . The man lifted her out and placed her on the ground on a blanket. Another man came up quickly, her father!

"Margo, Baby!" He gasped with disbelief at seeing his daughter. He was followed by another man wearing a hunter's red hat and clothes but carrying a doctor's bag.

And somehow, the sight of her father's face and the feel of the supporting earth helped. She felt safe.

"Daddy, the mill's on fire. It could burn the whole forest . . . Daddy!" But she felt weak and things were swimming before her eyes and she fell back on the blanket.

It was several hours before Margo gained consciousness. She woke to find herself in a bed in the Hunting Lodge. The same faces were before her. Her father and the man who must be a doctor. The sharp pain in her leg had gone and there was only a dull throb and it felt stiff. She glanced down to see it in a splint.

"How did Brian make it?" She still felt groggy.

The doctor spoke from beside her. "He's got a bad bump on his head but nothing seems to be broken. He must have been relaxed."

"He was." Margo laughed.

"I heard it on the radio, Baby," her father said. "The lookout reported the fire but the whole mill was ruined. I heard that Mr. Mac was found inside his home. He seemed dazed and incoherent. They've booked him on arson. I just can't believe Mac would . . ."

"He didn't, Dad." Margo felt her strength returning. Gradually she told her father and the doctor the story of Brian and the gasoline and the plane flight.

Margo's father smoothed the hair from her forehead and smiled down at her.

"Honey, you don't know how happy your old

Dad is to see you safe, and to know that it wasn't McAllister at all! As much as I hate to pay off claims, this is one claim I am going to be happy to pay."

Suddenly Margo remembered something. "What happened to Old Tony?"

"He was pulled out of the cutting shed when it was practically completely gone. He was in there trying to put out the fire with a little fire extinguisher. Lucky he wasn't killed. He just got minor burns."

Margo settled back with a great sense of safeness and asked, without any real concern, somehow, "What's wrong with my leg?"

The doctor spoke. "It's the small leg bone; the fibula. You'll be back in walking shape in no time."

Margo hardly heard him. Everything seemed right at last and a strange feeling of triumph spread through her like a healing warmth.

"Dad, could I . . . I mean when I'm over this . . ."

Her father must have been thinking the same thing. "Margo, do you know that you are a pretty remarkable woman to bring that plane over here and down on the field the way you did!"

"Well, now are you convinced?" she said. But what she meant was "See, now *I* am convinced."

"About what?"

"That I am as smart as a monkey?"

Her father tipped back his wide brimmed hat

156

and scratched his head. He chuckled softly. "You got me convinced, Honey. You just attend to healing up that leg and you can be sure some flying lessons will be waiting for you."

The Ghost Town Ghosts

◆ ◆ ◆ ◆

JACK WOOLGAR

JERRY Graham leaned back in the leather chair, stretched his long legs, and waited curiously for his uncle to speak. David, Jerry's younger brother, sat with eyes half closed. For a few moments the silence in the library was unbroken.

"I suppose," the gray haired man finally said, "you are wondering why I invited you here. I'll make it brief. I want you to investigate a ghost town."

Jerry straightened up, blue eyes puzzled. "A ghost town! Why?"

"Because I just bought one."

David opened his eyes lazily. "Any special ghost you want investigated?"

159

His uncle, Bill Graham, smiled. "No. Just find out if those ghosts are rumor or fact."

"Tell us more," Jerry said, eagerly. "Ghost hunting sounds like fun."

"It isn't funny to me," his uncle said, frowning. "I bought this abandoned mining town through my Arizona agent, with the intention of turning it into a tourist resort. Now I discover the place is haunted."

Jerry shrugged lean shoulders. "I don't believe in ghosts."

"Neither do I," Bill Graham said. "But as long as some tourists do, my investment is worthless. So if you two want to try and solve the mystery, I'll make it worth your while."

"We'll go," they chorused.

"It won't be easy. As a matter of fact, I was thinking of hiring professional investigators."

Jerry said, "I'm nineteen; Dave's seventeen. We're not kids."

"And don't think," Dave said, grinning, "that because I'm fat and a little lazy I can't get around. Boy, I'll move plenty fast if we really see ghosts."

Their uncle smiled and handed Jerry a letter. "Thought you would be interested, especially since it's your summer vacation. Here's instructions, money, and tickets to Yuma. My agent will furnish everything you need. I've spoken to your folks, so you can leave whenever you are ready. Good luck, and don't take unnecessary risks."

A few days later the brothers stepped off the train at Yuma. A stocky man wearing levis, flannel shirt, and tilted Stetson approached and held out his hand. "You must be the Graham brothers. I'm Joe Stillson. Welcome to Arizona."

They shook hands. Dave glanced at the agent's holsterless belt and said, "I thought everyone in Arizona wore six-shooters."

Joe showed white teeth in a smile. "Not in town. You'll need guns on the desert. Different clothes, too."

Jerry said, "What's the matter with our sports clothes? We're ghost hunters, not prospectors."

"You'll be in rough country," Joe said bluntly. "City clothes are out."

"Okay," Jerry said mildly. "Unc said you'd fix us up."

Joe did. Finally, dressed in western garb, they stowed the rest of their equipment in the agent's truck. It was two o'clock before they left Yuma and began their long trek to the ghost town. Joe, a former mountain guide, was not given to lengthy conversation, and for a time they rode in silence while the city boys admired the cacti studded scenery.

The ever inquisitive Jerry broke the silence. "Where is this spook town; what's its name?"

"'Bout hundred miles north, foot of Yapahav Mountain. Called Devil's Cash Box."

"Maybe that's what the ghosts are after. Cash." Dave said, yawning.

Joe grinned. "Mebbe. Used to be prosperous gold mine there. Petered out."

"Has it always been haunted?" Jerry asked.

"Nope. Not until real estate man bought it. Been haunted since. Even folks in nearby Adobe Junction stay away."

"How come the sheriff hasn't investigated?" Jerry persisted.

"Has. One night was enough. He ain't a timid man, either."

They turned off the highway onto the desert. Rutted tracks betrayed an ancient trail. The sun beat down relentlessly as purple mountains drew closer.

"Doesn't it ever cool off?" Dave grumbled, mopping his chubby face.

"Yep. Night time. You'll need blankets."

Jerry felt sweat trickle down his back, but he didn't complain. More serious than Dave, he began to realize they were not on a pleasure trip. They passed a lone shack.

"Ranger's place," Joe explained laconically. "You get in trouble, go there. Got two way radio."

The truck snaked along a sandy wash that led to a craggy mountain range. At its sloping base, a cluster of shacks became visible. No smoke curled upwards; nothing moved.

"There she is," Joe said abruptly.

They left the wash, rumbled up a rocky slope.

162

On their right a canyon split the mountain range. To their left, miners' shacks dotted the landscape in haphazard fashion. Straight ahead the deserted town loomed ominously. It consisted of one street, or road, with stores fronting both sides.

"Ghosts must be sleeping," Dave said.

"They'll wake up, come night," Joe predicted, dourly.

They chugged to the top of the slope and stopped on a plateau. It was a stone's throw away from the sinister looking street.

Joe said, "Better camp here. Safer. Anything creeps up, you can see and hear it."

Dave climbed out and stretched. "Any ghosts creep up, I'll be moving."

"Quit worrying," Jerry said, as he joined his brother. "You know there isn't any such thing as a ghost."

Dave grinned. "I do. But does the ghost know it?"

Joe was busy unpacking. After helping set up their tent, he made a sun shelter by piling creosote brush atop some palo verde saplings that he had chopped down.

"Gets plenty hot," he explained. "Best time for investigating is early morning or evening. Rest in daytime. Need help, call sheriff."

Dave looked at their supply of food and water. "We'll make out as long as rattlesnakes and ghosts leave us alone."

"Can't say about ghosts. Rattlers will give fair warning. Except side winders. Don't walk around in the dark."

"Thanks, Joe," Jerry said. "We appreciate your help. Maybe we'll find the ghosts before you return next week."

"Hope so," Joe grunted. "One more thing. When miners left, the Stiles family and Silent Smith stayed. After Stiles died, his daughter and three sons moved to the coast. Smith joined up with Cactus Charlie, an old prospector. Might still be around. Keep your eyes open. So long."

Washing down this long speech with a drink of water, Joe climbed into the truck and drove off. The two boys watched silently as the truck faded into the distance. Then they turned to stare at the Devil's Cash Box.

"Going in now?" Dave asked.

"Not until morning. If there's anyone hidden there, they've seen us by now. Let them make the first move. Besides, it will be dusk soon. Think I'll take a peek through our binoculars."

He saw a typical old time western street; about two dozen frame buildings, including a saloon, post office, livery stable, dance hall, and general store. The Yapahav Mountain, towering in majestic grandeur, was a shadowy backdrop.

"Simple layout," Dave observed. "The mountain and the main drag form a rough T. And speaking of tea, I'm thirsty and hungry. Let's eat."

164

Jerry grinned and lowered his glasses. "Might as well. Can't see anything moving. Probably siesta time for ghosts."

Dave opened some cans and they ate and watched the red sun bathe the mountain with splotches of liquid gold. The air began to lose its oppressive heat.

"Be dark soon," Jerry said. "Good thing we have lanterns and flashlights. We may need them."

"For snakes, maybe. Not ghosts. I need daylight to hunt them."

Jerry shrugged. "Ghosts don't bother me. I'm puzzled about a motive. There must be a reason for these illusions."

Night descended like a snuffed candle. One minute the mountain crest was tinted with brilliant color, then suddenly it was a jagged line against a purplish sky. A ghostly breeze sprang up, heavy with desert odors, and a pale moon crept over black peaks. Giant cacti cast weird shadows. The Devil's Cash Box was starkly mute; like a stage awaiting the actors.

A coyote howled, and closer a fox yapped. Loose rocks rattled down the canyon; touched off by small animals fleeing bigger ones. Dave shivered.

"Don't know if it's the air or the surroundings," he muttered, "but I'm cold. I'll get our jackets."

Thus protected against the chill air, they sat on camp stools and waited to see if ghosts would show. An hour passed. Two. Except for the coyote's mournful cry and the sounds of desert night life, there was nothing to disturb their vigil.

"Let's call it quits for tonight," Dave said, impatiently. "If anything happens, we'll hear it. Only Indians could crawl over these rocks without making a noise."

"Rattlesnakes could," Jerry said, flashing his light around. "But I guess you're right. We might as well . . ."

He stopped as lights suddenly blazed from windows on both sides of the street. A piano tinkled and from the blacksmith shop came the sound of hammer against anvil. High pitched voices and eerie laughter filled the air.

"Don't move!" Jerry whispered. "Let's see what else happens."

"Who's moving?" Dave groaned. "My legs are too shaky to run."

As suddenly as they came on, the lights went out and everything was quiet. Then a skeleton, wearing cowboy hat and boots, bounced out of the saloon. It slithered down the street and disappeared into the livery stable. Two more skeletons, groaning mournfully, staggered out of the dance hall and crossed the street into the general store. The lights winked on, the piano played chopsticks, and voices shrilled.

"M-maybe," Dave said shakily, "I'm dreaming. Maybe it's an illusion. Anyway, I'm scared."

"Does look spooky," Jerry admitted slowly. "But

there has to be a logical explanation. Come day-light, we're going to find out."

"If we're still here," Dave added.

"Then let's go now. I think it's a trick to frighten us."

"Far as I'm concerned," Dave said, "they've suc-ceeded. If you want to go down there, you go alone. I'm not tangling with skeletons."

Before Jerry could answer, the lights went out again and they heard deep throated barks. Up from the canyon raced half a dozen dogs, their white coats shedding a luminous glare. They fanned out into the ghostly street, wheeled, and bounded to-wards the two mystified watchers.

Dave drew his gun but Jerry clamped a hand on his wrist.

"Hold it, Dave! Hear that whistle?"

It shrilled again. Instantly the dogs whirled and were gone.

"Trained dogs," Jerry muttered. "What next?"

Dave holstered his gun. "Never knew ghosts had dogs. I'm getting more scared by the minute."

Jerry patted the younger boy's shoulder. "Stay with it, Dave. Your ghosts don't mean to harm us, or they wouldn't have called off those hostile hounds."

Suddenly a luminous white blob appeared part way up the dark mountain and floated to the ground. Down the street it glided and stopped op-posite the dance hall. The shapeless white figure was enough to frighten the most hardened skeptic. Then, in a shrill, quavering voice, the headless apparition screamed, "Go home, humans! This is your last warning!"

The ghostly figure turned slowly, glided back to the mountain, and vanished.

That was enough for Dave. Heedless of snakes, he made a beeline for their tent. Jerry, playing his flashlight ahead of him, followed. There was a puzzled frown on his face as he sank down on his cot.

"Know something, Dave? That last stunt left me a little edgy, too."

Dave threw aside a blanket and sat up. "Let's phone the sheriff tomorrow and have him pick us up. I'm not staying here a whole week. This place is haunted."

"We're not running away yet," Jerry said stoutly. "I'll admit things look spooky; they always do at night. But believe me, ghosts are a myth."

"That last one didn't myth us by much," Dave said, with a faint grin.

Jerry chuckled. "One more crack like that and I'll feed you to the ghosts. Now go to sleep. I think the show's over for tonight."

He poked his nose outside the tent. Overhead stars twinkled; a cool breeze was flushing the heat away. The Devil's Cash Box slept.

Early next morning they were roused by bees buzzing around the insulated water cans. After a hearty breakfast, Dave yawned and stretched. "Food always perks me up. Might even help you hunt ghosts, if it isn't too strenuous."

Jerry smiled. "Thought you'd feel different after a night's rest. Fill your canteen and we'll take off."

Just as they were ready to leave they heard a car in the canyon. It rattled around the turn, up the slope, and stopped along side them. A red faced man stepped out.

"Hiyah, boys!" he said, jovially. "Joe phoned and told me to keep an eye on you. I'm Tom Willard, Adobe Junction sheriff. How'd you make out last night?"

"Well, we're still here," Jerry said, shaking hands with the wiry, weather beaten sheriff. "But we saw plenty we can't explain."

"Can't explain what goes on here either," the sheriff grunted. "Figured maybe someone was playing tricks, but if they are, they're mighty clever. Like those lights. Miners took their generator away when they left."

"Might be another portable power unit around," Jerry said.

The sheriff shook his head. "Where would they hide it? Not in the mine. Main entrance on other side of mountain hasn't been used in years. Too dangerous. Used to be a tunnel from this side, but that's boarded up."

"Maybe the dogs shoot out electric sparks," Dave said, grinning.

"What dogs?" the sheriff demanded. "I never saw any; nearest ones are in Adobe, other side of mountain. Won't catch me here at night; I don't aim to get bit by no spook dog. Better watch out, boys. Even in daylight this place ain't healthy."

"You mean ghosts operate now?" Dave asked.

"Shore do. Not in the cabins; I combed them mighty careful. But they pulled some shenanigans in the saloon. Didn't harm me none, just made me jumpy like. Well, I'll be going. Things get too rough, give me a call. But not at night."

Jerry smiled. "Thanks, sheriff, but I guess we'll stick it out."

The sheriff shook his head and climbed into his car. With a wave of his hand, he drove away.

"Come on, Dave. Let's see these shenanigans he mentioned."

"I'll take his word for it, but if you insist . . ."

They walked slowly toward the deserted street. Lizards scuttled underfoot and pack rats rustled through the brush. Past the canyon on their right, dust devils spun and whirled.

The first shack bore a faded sign, U.S. Post Office. They opened a creaking door and stepped inside. Cobwebs festooned the ceiling and dust was inches thick. Jerry boldly explored the empty shack. It was evident that the place was unoccupied.

Across the way was another chipped sign, Red Dog Saloon. Jerry pushed past the batwing doors, with a reluctant Dave at his heels. Like the Post

Office, everything was covered with dust and cobwebs. All but the bar. The top had been cleaned
and glasses at one end were dust free. A cracked
mirror in back reflected Jerry's curious face.

Suddenly a glass slid down the bar as though
drawn by invisible hands. It toppled over the edge
and crashed to the plank floor.

"Wow!" Dave yelped. "Walking glasses!"

Jerry didn't answer. He was stooping over the
broken pieces. Baffled, he straightened up. "Figured it was a poltergeist trick, but no string. Beats
me."

There was a taunting laugh.

"More spooks," Dave mumbled. "Come on, Jerry. I'm not crazy about galloping glassware."

They walked out and stood in the dusty street.
"I'll tackle the dance hall," Dave said bravely. "But
if I find a ghost playing the piano, get out of my
way."

Jerry nodded absently and walked into the general store. The shelves were empty. He opened the
back door and looked out across the canyon. Just
as he turned away, a kerosene lamp that had been
on a rickety table, clattered to the floor. Jerry
whirled, found nothing but the broken lamp. He
scratched his head and walked out to meet Dave
coming from the dance hall.

"Find anything?"

"Not much. No dust on piano keys, if that means
anything."

"Means it was played by human beings," Jerry said. "Ghosts don't bother with dust."

Dave mopped his face. "And I don't bother ghosts."

The stalls in the livery stable were empty and so was the musty hayloft. A rusty pitchfork toppled over and Jerry said, "Poltergeists again. But how do you catch them?"

"I don't," Dave said promptly. "Any catching to be done, you do it."

Next door the blacksmith shop yielded another faint clue. No dust or cobwebs on the anvil. The chubby one looked unhappy.

"Let's go back, Jerry. I'm hot, hungry, and jumpy. Might feel better after we eat and rest."

Jerry glanced at his watch. "Almost noon. We'll go back, eat and pretend we're going to take a nap."

"Why pretend? I'm asleep already. Besides, it's too hot to hunt."

"That's what I want your ghosts to think," Jerry said, shrewdly. "Look, it's evident they watch every move we make. So when they see us enter our tent, they'll probably relax. Maybe we can surprise them."

"How do you expect to find ghosts when you don't know where to look?"

Jerry grinned. "I've got a hunch."

They continued silently to their tent. After a

hasty meal, they sprawled gratefully in the shade of the creosote brush.

"Here's how I figure it," Jerry began. "Unless they really are ghosts, they can't operate those lights without a power unit. We've got the sheriff's word that he couldn't find any in the cabins, and we've searched both sides of the street. What's left? The mine."

"With one entrance boarded up and the other unsafe," Dave mocked.

Jerry nodded. "So they must have a secret entrance on this side. We'll wait an hour and then slip out the back of our tent into that little wash behind us. We'll follow that until we get above and to the west of the cabins. Then we hug the base of the mountain and work east. We're bound to find something."

"You hope," Dave grumbled, as he tumbled into the tent. In a few minutes he was sound asleep.

An hour later Jerry shook him awake and they began their stealthy climb up the wash and over the rocky slope behind the cabins. The sun blazed down and the water in their canteens was warm. Twice snakes slithered across their path and once Dave almost stepped on a Gila monster. When they finally gained the mountain base, they stopped to rest.

Then, slowly, carefully, they worked their way east towards the Devil's Cash Box. They scanned crevices, watched sandy spots for footprints. When they reached the last row of cabins, Jerry paused. "Must have missed it on the way down. Let's go back."

They had gone only a short distance when Dave spotted it; a mere slit between the mountain and a ledge of rock. Jerry squeezed in first and after a few steps saw the opening. Heavy timbers shored the sides, and the tip of a ladder was visible. He beckoned to Dave, and the two boys stared down the dark hole.

"Now what? Do we drag the ghosts out or pounce on them when they come up?"

Jerry wiped his forehead and grinned. "Got to find them first. Let's hope they're napping."

They unhooked miners' lanterns from their belts and, one by one, climbed down to a rocky shelf. A ramp, large enough for them to walk upright, descended to a dank smelling tunnel.

"Quiet now," Jerry whispered. "We don't want to warn them."

They entered the tunnel and looked around in awe. To their left, flickering lantern beams glinted on various colored veins. A pile of freshly mined ore blocked the passage. To their right the tunnel stretched away parallel to the mountain above them. The silence was oppressive.

After a short distance they came to a cross tunnel. Jerry stopped. There was a satisfied look on his face. He glanced around cautiously, as though expecting to find something. His eyes sparkled when he saw the ladder.

"Wait here," he whispered. "I'll be right back."

Jerry ascended the ladder which led, as he expected, to an opening boarded on the outside. Nails had been sheared off and replaced by hooks on the inside. He lifted the hooks quietly and the boards slid outward on well greased hinges. He looked south, straight into the Devil's Cash Box lone street.

He smiled grimly, re-hooked the boards, and climbed down. "Come on," he whispered. "Our ghosts can't be far away."

They turned into the southbound tunnel. The air smelled fresher and supporting beams betrayed no sign of age. A short distance ahead they saw a faint light. They switched off their lamps.

Cautiously they crept forward until Jerry was able to see the opening. Then he stepped boldly into the entrance of a natural cave.

"May we come in, Ma'am?" he asked politely.

There was a startled gasp and a dark haired girl, dressed in levis and rough shirt, jumped up from a stool. Her tanned, young face was dirt-smudged as she faced Jerry defiantly.

"Who are you? How did you find us?" she demanded.

Jerry, with an astonished Dave behind him, moved into the light cast by a single hanging bulb. He smiled pleasantly.

"I'm Jerry Graham, and this is my brother Dave.

He discovered your secret entrance. Now, Miss Stiles, why all this spook business?"

Suddenly three boys, brown as Indians and ranging in age from ten to fifteen, brushed aside a dividing curtain and blinked sleep from their eyes.

"Hi, fellows!" Jerry said, grinning. "We were just asking about ghosts. Maybe you'd like to tell us."

"I'll talk," the girl said, wearily. "All right. I'm Sue Stiles and these are my brothers, Bill, Harry, and Jim. We rigged up fake ghosts to keep strangers away."

"But why?"

"Because the Cash Box is the only home we know," she said, stubbornly. "We told the sheriff and Adobe folks that we were moving to the coast after Pa died, but we sneaked back here during the night."

Jerry looked curiously around the homelike cave. "How about school for your brothers?"

"Had some schooling myself and taught the boys. We read a lot. That's how I got the idea for ghosts."

"Books and food cost money. Where does that come from?"

She sighed. "Might as well tell you, since you've found us. Silent Smith and Cactus Charlie are still mining a little gold out of the west spur. They share it with us. Cactus hauls in supplies from Adobe Junction."

"They help you dig this tunnel, rig up lights?"

Sue nodded. "Bought a portable power unit and Smith did the wiring. Now I suppose you'll tell the sheriff and he'll make us leave."

Dave suddenly found his voice. "We don't need to tell anyone, Miss Stiles. You see, our uncle wants to convert this town into a tourist resort. Why can't you and your brothers stay on as caretakers?"

Jerry smiled approval. "You can even live in a remodeled miner's cabin. So let's shake hands and bury the ghosts."

Shyly, Sue and the boys shook hands.

"Now," Jerry exploded, "will you please explain a few things. I can guess some of it, but not all."

She smiled. "First, I've got a question. How did you know my name?"

"I didn't. But it was a good guess, since I'd heard that you used to live here."

"How did you find our hideout?" piped up freckle faced Bill.

"Looked for it," Jerry said, grinning. "Almost missed it too."

"No wonder the dogs didn't bark," Sue said. "They're inside the main entrance on the other side. We keep them there in case strangers started to explore. It's safer than people think, even though the beams are rotting."

"How about starting at the beginning?" Dave said. "I'm dumber than Jerry."

"We all helped extend the tunnel underneath the street. Cactus helped Smith with the wiring, includ-

177

ing amplifiers and microphones. Took a long time, because we didn't want the sheriff to catch on."

"Were you all those voices?" Jerry asked.

"Mostly. Smith and Cactus helped. The boys blackened their hands and faces and wore black suits with white bones painted on for their skeleton acts. I made luminous outfits for the dogs and trained them to answer a whistle."

Jerry nodded. "The stuff that fell over. I couldn't find any string."

"Boys used black thread with big loops so they could be jerked off. Ran thread through holes in the wall and operated them from outside."

"Weren't they afraid of being caught?"

Bill snickered. "You opened a door but didn't see me. I'm pretty good at ducking around this old town."

"How about the piano and anvil? Strings too?"

"No. The boys hopped in the back way before the lights went on, and left the same way. Hard to see them with black suits."

Jerry chuckled. "I thought chopsticks was a funny tune for a ghost. Well, that explains everything except your most brilliant effort. The floating ghost."

The four Stiles grinned broadly. Sue said, "That was Cactus Charlie's idea. I wore a white sheet with black lining; easy to become visible or invisible on a dark mountain. I climbed up a trail to where a rope was stretched from a rock to a stake in the ground. Slipped the sheet, white side out, over my head and slid down the rope in a sling. Harry removed the rope and sling soon as I was down."

"Scared the daylights out of me," Dave said ruefully.

"Scared the sheriff too," Sue said demurely.

Jerry laughed. "Wish I could tell the sheriff, just to watch his face."

"Please don't," she begged.

"I won't let him," Dave assured her, "although it wouldn't really matter. Unc will probably be appointed your guardian, and the boys may have to go to school. But you're free right now to climb out of this cave."

"I'll be glad to live in a house again," she said. "How long are you staying?"

"Long enough for you to guide us around this fantastic desert and mountain," Jerry answered.

She nodded shyly. "Be glad to. But remember, not a word to the sheriff."

Jerry winked at Dave. "The ghost town ghosts are dead. That's all he'll ever know. We aren't going to admit that we were fooled by a girl."

29639 SHE WANTED TO READ: *The Story of Mary McLeod Bethune*, by Ella Kaiser Carruth. Illustrated by Herbert McClure. A biography about the famous black educator who was born in South Carolina in 1875 and became a world-acclaimed college president and civic leader. (75¢)

29718 SECRET OF THE INDIAN MOUND, by Wilson Gage. Illustrated by Mary Stevens. While helping their uncle dig for treasures in an old burial mound, Alec and Jimmy also stir up an unexpected mystery. (95¢)

29771 MISHMASH, by Molly Cone. Illustrated by Leonard Shortall. Life is full of surprises for Pete when he gets Mishmash—a huge, black, friendly hound who turns the whole town topsy-turvy with his hilarious doings. (95¢)

29802 SEA MONSTERS, written and illustrated by Walter Buehr. A fascinating discussion of the myths, facts, and scientific theories about the existence of giant sea creatures from prehistoric times to the present. ($1.25)

29309 DANNY DUNN *and the Smallifying Machine*, by Jay Williams and Raymond Abrashkin. Illustrated by Paul Sagsoorian. When Danny gets trapped in Professor Bullfinch's latest invention, he shrinks to insect size and must face survival in a world that has become a giant jungle. (60¢)

29755 THE GHOST OF FIVE OWL FARM, by Wilson Gage. Illustrated by Paul Galdone. During school vacation Ted and his twin cousins set out to investigate the weird goings-on in an old barn —including a headless shape that glows in the dark. (95¢)

29747 ENCYCLOPEDIA BROWN SAVES THE DAY, by Donald J. Sobol. Illustrated by Leonard Shortall. Match wits with America's Sherlock Holmes in Sneakers as he takes on ten exciting new cases, finds the clues, and solves the crimes. (95¢)

29740 THE TRUE STORY OF OKEE THE OTTER, by Dorothy Wisbeski. Illustrated with photographs. The beloved pet of a suburban family, Okee is a happy-go-lucky clown, curious about everything, and in and out of mischief. ($1.25)

29765 THREE ON THE RUN, by Nina Bawden. Frontispiece illustration by Wendy Worth. Sudden adventure grips Ben, Lil, and their African friend, Thomas Okapi, as they are plunged into an international plot and must make a wild, desperate flight from London. ($1.25)

(If your bookseller does not have the titles you want, you may order them by sending the retail price, plus 25¢ (50¢ if you order two or more books) for postage and handling to: Mail Service Department, POCKET BOOKS, a division of Simon & Schuster, Inc., 1 West 39th Street, New York, N. Y. 10018. Please enclose check or money order—do not send cash.)

75747